HOBO COWBOY

JACK OVERBEY

Copyright © 2018 Jack Overbey
All rights reserved
First Edition

PAGE PUBLISHING, INC.
New York, NY

First originally published by Page Publishing, Inc. 2018

ISBN 978-1-64138-966-2 (Paperback)
ISBN 978-1-64138-968-6 (Hardcover)
ISBN 978-1-64138-967-9 (Digital)

Printed in the United States of America

INTRODUCTION and DEDICATION

I introduce this book with pride and humility. Some may say the introduction is too long, but I disagree. It's not long enough. I'm dedicating this book to my father and to my readers.

John Martin Overbey, my father, was born on December 24, 1901, in a log cabin on a hillside farm in Laurel County, Kentucky. He was a man among men. I remember as a child, he would take me fishing at night on the Local River for catfish. Only he and I were there. He had nine children and raised two additional grandchildren. I guess I was the most adventurous one of them all. He and I spent a lot of time together. This is only one of the times we've made that wonderful trip to the old fishing hole. He would always bring along a cast-iron number 12 skillet, a little lard, some cornmeal, which we grew and had ground ourselves, shake up the catfish in the meal after they had been cleaned, fry them to a golden brown along the banks of the river—nothing could have tasted better. We would build a small fire close to the water and wait for the catfish to bite.

We would sit around the fire, and Dad would tell me some of his adventures as a young hobo, on his ventures west. I was all ears with wide eyes and an open mind and heart. Many of the incidents in this book are Dad's true travels. He did have a cousin named Robert Chestnut, who hoboed west and worked on a ranch in Eastern Oregon. His cousin was shot and killed by supposedly a blank cartridge when he was driving a stage coach during a fake holdup at a local rodeo. He was killed because he was top rodeo performer among all the ranches in the vicinity. The competition was fierce. I grew up riding his saddle, which was sent to dad in Kentucky after his cousin was murdered. The other cowboys were jealous of him. Dad did work on the irrigation ditch, in Weiser, Idaho, and he did have a partner die of a rattlesnake bite while working on the canal. He learned to shoot a .38 pistol with excellent marksmanship and speed. He could drive a nail into a post or tree from fifty feet with one shot. I saw him do it many times in competition. And yes, he did sell harvested game to the local restaurants and saloons. There were two horses named Wigwam and Papoose.

On Saturday midafternoon when his work was over, he was the local iceman who delivered chunks of ice for ice boxes. In those days, there were very few refrigerators, and Dad would carry twenty-five to fifty to seventy-five or a hundred pounds of ice up the steps to replenish his customer's ice boxes. It was a tiring grueling job, but he had mouths to feed. On Saturday after a hard week's work, he would take my small hand in his large calloused hand, and we would walk up to the ticket booth of the lyric theater. They only showed Westerns, like Tom Mix, Tim Holt, Johnny Mack Brown, Bob Steele, Hopalong Cassidy, Lash Larou, and Red Ryder. He would buy two ten-cent tickets and two five-cent bags of buttered popcorn. He'd look down at me and say, "Let's go ride with the cowboys, Jack." And we did. Thanks, Dad.

Listening to the clickety-clack of the boxcar wheels on the wet rails is mesmerizing. Even with the rust-colored sliding door closed, the cold wind and smoke from the wood-fired engine is creeping into the boxcar, reaching inside my flimsy coat and making me cold down to my toes. It is early spring but still very cold. It would be beyond endurance if my beagle hound dog was not snuggling up to me, giving me some of his warmth. His name is Major. I raised him from a pup and taught him almost everything he knows, but he has a lot of natural instincts and talents all by himself.

I can smell the pungent, lingering odors of the damp interior of the boxcar and the many cargoes that it has carried. I can smell the grain on the floor spilled from the grain sacks, the cattle, the horses, and the hogs that were once transported in this boxcar. I can see the ashes of a small fire that the previous traveler or bum had built trying to stay warm. He had built a fire on an old, rusty piece of metal so it wouldn't catch the boxcar on fire. I am hoping that the railroad detective (or bull) doesn't find me, as they—for the most part—are pretty violent men, by necessity.

I'm a little over sixteen years old and about six feet tall. I may grow some yet—broad shoulders with slim hips; light, sandy hair; and blue eyes—and I could take care of myself in a scuffle. I left my home to see the west. I decided riding the rails was the best course of action as I had no other means of transportation—no money, no horse, nothing. My mother died when I was born, and Dad married another woman, who helped him raise me. But her heart wasn't in the chore or for my well-being. Taking care of me was not something that she wanted to do. I wasn't her son! My father was killed eight months ago, and my stepmother decided I was too grown up to stay on the family farm. I think she has a boyfriend! So I left. I'd say she really ran me off the place. In my early years at home with my father, he told me about his young years hoboing to the west and shared some of his experiences on the rails. So here I am in this frigid boxcar heading west—no money, nothing to eat, no place to sleep (except a little loose hay that I piled up in the most protected corner of the boxcar) or call home—just me and Major.

In my growing-up years, I didn't have a lot of entertainment. Our farm was so far back in the hills that they had to pump daylight to us. So after I had done my chores on the farm, I decided that I wanted to be a person who could handle and throw a knife well. So that was my entertainment. With dad's help—he was pretty handy with a forge—we fashioned two throwing knives that I still have. One knife I keep just below the hairline on my neck and under the collar of my shirt in a sheath on a leather thong. The other knife, I keep in a sheath on my belt. I have practiced throwing these two knives quickly—very quickly—and accurately, sometimes both knifes at the same time. As a young boy, I fantasized how I would defend myself and my family with these two knives, if it ever came to that. The constant work and practice with the knives, I believe, has paid me huge dividends.

I could feel the train slowing down, so I slid open the boxcar door slightly, and I saw a town in the distance. It was cold outside, and I could see the wood and coal smoke hanging over the town. I could hear someone running on the roof of my boxcar, and I saw shadows from the roof, reflecting on the railbed. Men were running and climbing down the steel steps from the break wheel, some jumping off the train and rolling over and over, trying to escape the large bully club that belonged to the railroad dick (or bull). I checked the lay of the land on my side of the track, opened the door wider, took Major in my arms, and jumped. I held Major tight in my arms, hoping he wouldn't break any bones. He is so important to me especially at this time in my life. He is the only link to my former life. We finally stopped rolling, coming to a stop up against a large rock. My head was reeling from the blow. I moved my body slowly, seeing if I or Major was hurt. I found a few scrapes and minor cuts but no broken bones, and neither did Major. We blended into the thick brush of blackberry vines along the side of the track. I could hear some of the other hobos running and thrashing through the brush to get clear of the railroad bull's club. These hobos are men I came to know, out of work, down on their luck, riding the rails looking for a work opportunity—which did no harm to the railroads, but the railroad still didn't want them riding the boxcars. Some of them were humble men who had to leave their families to find work. Some of them believed that the world owed them a living, and some of them were running from the law.

They were all running for a location that I soon learned was the hobo jungle (camp). The number of hobos at the jungle fluctuated. Some went to town to panhandle; some went to find work; some went to find sympathetic sawbones (doctor) who would treat their ills for free; and some hitched rides on other trains. It was a constant flux. There were all kinds of men and women. Some were highly educated, and some had no schooling whatsoever, except the school of hard knocks. Each had his or her own story to tell, which most of the time they kept to themselves.

But there was one hobo who interested me. His name was Will, and I learned later a hobo term for him was *cattle stiff*. He was a cowboy down on his luck. He had a cowboy hat (which used to be white), a pair of Levi pants, a cowboy shirt with a torn vest pocket, cowboy boots with a hole in the sole, and overrun heels on his boots. In other words, he looked the part of a man down on his luck—at least what you would imagine a hobo looked like. But when his eyes looked at you, the goodness showed through. He was riding the rails trying to find a cowpoke job. Some called it a grub line. He had been a cowboy since early childhood. He had a gat (pistol) in a holster on his hip with a few bullets in the belt. He was friendly enough, but most of the hobos kept their distance. Some time ago, Will had to sell his horse and saddle to pay for his keep, and he was, you might say, depressed and stayed mostly to himself. I came into the jungle knowing no one; you can imagine that I treaded very softly.

There was some mulligan stew bubbling over an open fire. Mulligan is made up of anything edible—and some things I would hardly call edible—that you can find: chicken, rabbit, carrots, turnips, beans, anything thrown into the same pot and let cook. Each hobo, if he could, would gather from various locations food to add to the stew and give it to the mess moll (a woman cook for the jungle).

One of the hobos saw Major and decided that he would be good to put in the mulligan stew since it had no meat.

I said, "No deal. This is my dog, leave him alone."

There was some argument about eating dog, but one of the hobos said that the Western Indian tribes ate dog. Several tribes were called dog eaters, and if it was good enough for the Indian tribes, it was good enough for him as he grabbed Major. Some of the Indian tribes that ate dog were Teton Sioux, Paiutes, Nez Perce, Cheyenne. They raised dogs for food. They would not eat wolf, as they thought it was sacred. The Aztec empire bred the Mexican hairless dogs for food. It was a delicacy allocated for the king.

Quicker than the eye could see, I pulled my knife out of the sheath on my hip and threw it at the hobo holding Major, hitting him in the shoulder and going deep into his flesh. He dropped Major on the ground. He was hollering like a banshee.

I said, "I told you to leave my dog alone."

Some of the other hobos started walking toward me. Will stood up and pulled his .38 cal. pistol and said, "Leave the kid and his dog alone."

They backed away fast. I went over and jerked my knife out of the hobo's shoulder, wiped the blood off on his shirt, and put it back in my sheath.

I walked over to Will, shook his hand, and said, "Thanks for your help. My name is Bill Chestnut."

Will said, "You're awful sudden with that knife, Bill."

"Some," I said, with a grim look on my face. "He shouldn't have been threatening my dog."

Will said, "I don't believe they'll do that again right soon."

I told Will that Major and I were going for a walk to try and sort things out—where I was, where I wanted to go, the best way to accomplish those things, and just generally think about the situation and clear my mind. I called Major, and we started our journey. In about ten minutes of walking, either Major or I scared up a rabbit. It was a cottontail, not a jackrabbit. Jackrabbits are much larger than a cottontail, but the meat is tough and stringy. Major started running after the rabbit as fast as he could. He occasionally barked to let me know his location as he did back on the farm. Most of the time, a rabbit—if he is not hard-pressed—will run in a left-handed circle and come back to the same area where he was before being disturbed, so I stood and waited, believing the rabbit would return and I could kill it with my knife. This race between Major and the rabbit lasted about fifteen minutes, and then I heard Major's bark. And I knew he was not on the trail but had treed the rabbit. It either had gone into a hole in the ground or had gotten into a rotten hole in a tree, so I started toward the bark. Major's bark let me know that he had the rabbit treed. It didn't matter if it was in a tree or in a hole in the ground or a rock. The different bark said he had it stopped but couldn't get at the rabbit.

I found Major at the trunk of the tree that had a large hole in the bottom, and it looked as if the hole was maybe four feet inside the large tree trunk. On the farm, hunting with Dad, he taught me how to twist a rabbit out of a hole, either on the ground or in a tree trunk or in a rock. It didn't matter. It was a tried-and-true method. I cut myself a willowy limb off the nearest tree and made a *Y* off of one of the limbs growing at the end. I stuck the willow limb in the hole and pushed it in until I could go no farther, and I twisted a couple of turns and then brought the tree limb out of the hole and took a look at the end, and there on the fork was rabbit fur. I knew for sure that Major had run the rabbit into this whole. I put my willow stick back in the hole up to the end and twisted and twisted and twisted it into the fur of the rabbit until it became difficult to twist any longer, and I started pulling the willow limb out of the hole, and I could hear the rabbit's claws trying desperately to withstand the pulling effect of my limb.

I pulled the rabbit almost out of the hole, far enough that I could grab one of its legs, and then I continued pulling it out until the entire rabbit was in my hand. I dispatched it quickly and hung it on my belt. Major and I continued our walk and scared up another rabbit. This time I sat on a rock close to where the rabbit had jumped up and waited. Sure enough, the rabbit came back. It had taken a left turn and made a circle, and I saw it hopping slowly back to where it had sat before.

You know, a beagle has short legs, and they can't run really fast enough to catch a rabbit. They are made perfect to be a rabbit and squirrel dog as they have a good nose and can smell the scent but are not fast enough to catch either animal.

As the rabbit got closer, I pulled my knife and waited. When he got close enough, I threw the knife and added another rabbit to my belt.

I returned to the hobo jungle and gave the two rabbits to the mess moll so she could add them to the mulligan stew. I told the camp that this was my and Will's contribution to our share of the stew. She was glad to get them. I told Will that I was going into town the next day to try and find some work. If he wanted to go with me, he would be welcome. Will decided that was a good idea. We would go in the town and try and find something useful to do. Both he and I needed some money to live on and to buy a horse and saddle. I knew Will missed working on a ranch and was desperately trying to find that type of work.

After eating our share of the stew, we settled in for the night under the stars. It was a miserable night trying to stay warm and dry from the misty, cold rain that had been falling since late evening. But in the morning, the sky was clear, and we had a different outlook on life. Surprising what the sun can do to a man's disposition.

That morning, Will and I and, of course, Major made tracks into town, looking for work. We decided—since I was raised on a farm and knew a little about cattle and horses and Will had worked on a ranch most of his life—we should maybe go to the local livery stable and see if he had work or knew of someone that needed help.

The elderly man who ran the livery was very easy to talk to, and we told him our dire circumstances. We told him that we did not enjoy riding the rails and living the life of a hobo, that we wanted substantial jobs if it was available anywhere in the area. He said that he sympathized with our predicament, but the livery stable wasn't making a lot of money. But he would hire us for the day to muck out, clean out the stalls, and stack hay and pay each of us fifty cents a day and food.

We said, "Okay, that's more than we have now," and we went to work and vowed to do him a decent job.

A longtime customer came into the stable and wanted his horse saddled. He was going for an important ride. As he was riding out the livery gate, a bunch of rowdies from a nearby ranch came riding and running their horses past the stable, shooting their guns in the air and spooking every horse along the Main Street, including the horse of the longtime customer. His horse wasn't gentle broke, and it started bucking and rearing up almost to the point where it would go over backward. Will jumped into action, grabbed the horse's reins, and I pulled the rider off the horse and put him along the fence in a safe place so he wouldn't get trampled. The horse was excited but soon calmed down under Will's soothing voice. We told the rider that we were sorry, that we only wanted to help and to keep him from getting hurt.

He said, "No apology necessary. If it wasn't for you two, I may have gotten really hurt. If the horse had fallen backward with me in the saddle, it would have been disastrous."

The livery owner had seen the whole thing. He told his customer that we were only working at the livery for the day because we were out of work, and we had told him our hard-luck story.

The customer listened and said, "Would you two saddle up horses, I'll pay for the rental, and ride with me for a spell?"

The livery owner said he had two special horses that he would rent to us. Their names were Wigwam and Papoose. We saddled the horses and met our benefactor at the livery gate. He told us that he was riding out to the Weiser, Idaho, Washington County irrigation ditch—quite a mouthful to talk to two of his employees. The county ditch was sold to him in 1886 for $10,000, and he was having a problem getting the employees to do their job. He asked Will and me if we would be interested in taking on longtime employment. We looked at each other and said yes.

He said, "Okay, let's look this job over and see if you're interested." He said, "The pay is one dollar a day each," and found that that was music to our ears.

He also said that we were furnished a tent and all the ammunition that we wanted for our weapons, he would let us use them for free.

He said, "By the way, my name is Jim Galloway, but you can call me Jim."

We reached the irrigation canal and followed it about a half mile to the location of the employee's camp. We found them sitting around drinking coffee.

They stood up and greeted Mr. Galloway cordially and said, "Hello, boss."

"Men," said Mr. Galloway, "I'm here to inspect the irrigation ditch. I have reports on my desk that the ditch has not stayed clean and water is not flowing freely. I hired you men to keep the canal clean and move your campsite up and down the canal, cleaning it as you travel. I have brought these gentlemen to be your replacements, if what the report says is true, and from where I'm standing now, it looks like it is true."

I was thinking that this situation could become dicey, so I backed my horse about ten feet to the left and looked at Will, and he was doing the same thing to the right. He and I were on the same mind track. Mr. Galloway told the men to pack up their gear and go back to town and meet at his office; he would give them their pay. He told them to turn in the weapons to him now.

One of the men said, "Maybe we will, and maybe we won't, we've gotten used to these weapons," and his hand darted down toward his pistol.

Quick as a wink, I pulled my knife from behind my neck and in one fluid motion threw the knife into his forearm, and he dropped the weapon back into his holster. In fact, he never even got the pistol completely out of his holster. By that time, Will had his weapon out and was covering the other employee. Mr. Galloway gathered up the weapons and all visible ammunition and put it in his saddlebags.

He said, "Boys, this is the second time today that you saved my bacon from bodily harm, I won't forget."

Mr. Galloway then asked if we two wanted the job of keeping the canal clean and water flowing.

We said, "Most assuredly, yes."

We told him that we needed to go get our gear and bring it to the campsite and turn in the horses.

Mr. Galloway said, "No, you keep these horses for your use. I'll pay the bill at the livery, go get your gear and let's start work."

We went with Mr. Galloway back to town to the emporium. I picked out a .45 caliber pistol, holster and ammo. Will chose ammunition for his .38, and we got the other goods that we needed to start work: coffeepot, Arbuckle coffee, bacon, beans, jerky, some airtight canned tomatoes, canned peaches, canned pears, cooking pot, dishes, and a few minor things. Mr. Galloway told the clerk to put all on his bill and to give us whatever we needed as time went on.

In returning to the campsite, we cleaned up the other men's residue that they had left behind and threw our bedrolls into the tent. I put my pistol around my waist and loaded it, and we decided to go for a walk, maybe a mile up the canal and then maybe a mile down the canal, to get our bearings and to understand what our job was going to be. As we walked along the canal, we saw signs of wild animals. There was deer, bear, elk, mountain lion. I could see why we needed to have our weapons with us at all times. All wild animals needed the water in this canal. This water would attract wild animals like bees to honey. This could be a dangerous profession if you didn't watch your peas and cues.

We decided that we would give Mr. Galloway our best effort in doing the proposed irrigation canal job. Will and I knew that we would be alone out here camping along the canal—subject to any roving outlaw, hobos, or any rowdy cowboys in the vicinity. We must expect some trouble and be prepared at any given time. That first night on the job, it rained, and we were glad we had the tent to keep us dry—better than the hobo jungle and sleeping out under the stars. I don't know if Will missed it or not, but I sure didn't. We picketed our horses on the side of the canal where the water had seeped through and green grass grew a couple of feet tall along the canal for a short distance. They were completely satisfied, and of course, Major stayed in the tent with us.

The next day we began our job of filling any leaks in the dirt canal and cutting wild growth that was growing and impeding the water flow and using up the water. Keeping a good flow of water was our main job so the farmers downstream could grow their needed crops.

When our daily work was done, I asked Will if he would teach me to shoot and pull an iron out of the holster fast. I had seen him before at the hobo jungle and knew that he could pull a gun fast. I felt it was my obligation to him and Jim Calloway to know how to draw a fast gun.

So each day, or almost each day, we used up a lot of Mr. Galloway's free ammunition. Sometimes in the early morning, Major would alert us that a wild animal was in our vicinity, and we would try to get some fresh camp meat. About a quarter of the time, we were successful in getting a deer or an occasional elk for our soup pot. The eating was good. The only problem was, we had to do our own cooking, not like the camp mess moll back at the jungle.

When we were able to harvest a deer or an elk, we would take a nice quarter over to Jim Galloway and a quarter or more to the hobo jungle to feed the people there, and they were very grateful. We had made a deal with the local restaurant and saloon to bring them fresh meat for their customers, and they would pay us for the meat. Will and I would try and save the money that we got from the restaurants to buy some gear to travel West. We did not intend that this canal job would be permanent, but we did appreciate Jim Galloway giving us this opportunity to get on our feet and to make plans for the future. We would move our camp about every two weeks—a couple of miles down the canal, a couple of miles up the canal, depending where we were needed most. Sometimes we would have to get into the water and cut wild brush completely out of the canal, from the bottom of the canal.

In our talking, sitting around the campfire in the evenings, I told Will that I had a first cousin who came out West when he was a young man, and he got a job on a cattle ranch in eastern Oregon.

"His name is Robert Chestnut. Word has gotten back to our hometown that he is an excellent cowboy. He is the best bronc rider, bull rider, and just an all-around best cowboy based on the local rodeos. There was always competition between the ranches. He works for the Double O Bar Ranch. One of these days I want to go look him up. In my very young years, he and I were friends. He's dad's brother's boy. The competing ranch in the area is the Rafter Bar, and they were always trying to best Robert in all the competition events, but Bobby still holds the trophies."

With all the practicing that we were doing with our weapons, we were fast becoming excellent shots—I, with my .45 caliber pistol, and Will, with his .38. I would hit my target almost every time, and Will could do the same. We could be formidable adversaries if it came to that. We could take a horseshoe nail and hit it with a hammer lightly to start it into a tree trunk and back off fifty to sixty feet and hit the nail with the first shot and drive the nail into the trunk; now that is pretty good shooting. My fast draw was coming along well also.

With the money that we had saved selling the meat to the restaurants and saloons, we had enough to go to the emporium and buy us each a Henry rifle with a fifteen-shot magazine. I chose a .357 Magnum, and Will chose the 3006. It wouldn't hold fifteen rounds, but it held enough. We each took one hundred rounds of ammunition. We told Jim Galloway what we had done, putting the ammo on his bill to pay. He was okay with that.

Mr. Galloway came to visit, and I guess really to inspect the work that we are doing, but I don't think he had any complaints because we were doing the best job that we knew how. I asked Mr. Galloway what was going to happen in the wintertime, since the farmers wouldn't be growing crops that time of year. He said that he was going to have to cut down on his employees, but he didn't want to do that to Will and me. I told him that I would like to take some time off this winter and go see my cousin who was working at the Double O Bar Ranch and get reacquainted with him. He said, that was a good idea, that he approved, and we could leave as soon as he brought another employee here to take our place temporarily. That sounded okay to Will and me. It was starting to get a little cool at night, but it wasn't freezing yet.

He brought another employee by the name of Ray (I never knew his last name) to our camp about a week later and said, "This is your winter replacement, so show him the ropes, and you and Will can leave at your convenience. Come by and pick up your money when you leave."

The next day we took Ray with us and showed him what the job entailed. We had been walking along the canal bank for some time. Ray suggested that we get a drink. I told him there was a spring a little further up the canal that had cool water and we would get a drink there, which suited him fine.

Upon reaching the spring, I showed Ray the spring, and he knelt down to get a drink. No one saw the coiled rattlesnake on the edge of the spring. As Ray lowered his head toward the water, the rattlesnake struck, biting Ray on the forehead, almost between his eyes. I told Will to ride fast to town and bring the doctor. Maybe there was still hope for Ray. I took my knife, made an X cut on the snakebite, and tried to suck the venom out of the bite. The cut was bleeding profusely, and I thought that might help flush the venom out. I tried to keep Ray still, but it was hopeless. He knew what was happening. His face was swelling; his eyelids were swelling rapidly; and he could not see very well. And that was adding to his fear of the snakebite. I did all I knew, but I had a feeling down deep that Ray would not survive this attack. I shot the head of the snake while waiting for the doctor and Will to return.

The sawbones (doctor) came, but it was too late for Ray. I believe he was dead when the doctor arrived. It was a sad thing, but when you were living out in the wilds, as we were, serious things could happen unexpectedly. We reported the death of Ray to the sheriff and to Jim Galloway. We took the body back into town to the undertaker, and Jim told the undertaker that he would pay for burying Ray.

Jim also said, "Boys, it will take me maybe a week to find someone to take Ray's place, so if you can hang out doing the job for another week, I would appreciate it."

We had no place to go except back to our tent on the canal bank and continue the job. We were sort of low thinking of Ray and that it might have been my fault for taking him to the spring.

We did talk to the livery owner before we went back to camp and asked him how much Wigwam and Papoose would cost, including the saddles, bridles, saddle blankets, and so on. We didn't know if we had enough money saved to buy the horses or not for a trip West to find my cousin. If needed, we would have to ride the rails again and take our chances with the railroad bulls. Of course, we were better armed and could handle our weapons better than last time, but we didn't want to kill anyone.

When Galloway brought the second employee to take our place, he asked us to do the same as we had for Ray—of course, minus the snakebite. The new man had already heard the story, as we told him some of the dangers living in the wilds. We told him that he could harvest some of the game and sell it to the restaurants and the saloon as we had and make a little extra money; it was his choice. After we had shown the new man around, we decided to collect our pay and head West. We wanted to get to Eastern Oregon before the snow flew. We didn't have enough money to buy Wigwam or Papoose, so we went to the hobo jungle to say goodbye and find the best train to hop to get to our destination. The hobos knew the bulls on all of the trains, and we asked them the best train to get to our destination. They said the train to hop is Old Great Northern and that the bull on that train was violent and enjoyed using his club, so be careful. They were our friends since we had been giving them harvested meat for their mulligan stew. They were sad to see us go—maybe because the meat would stop; the new canal employee had no ties with the jungle as we did. We decided to hop the train after it had left the town, not before—maybe the bull would be settled down and not be on the prowl.

I had spoken to another hobo about boarding the Old Great Northern Railroad. He said the train was going to stop for water about three miles north of town. With that in mind, we decided to walk there and board the train while they were taking on water. We were trying to avoid a dustup with the railroad bull. We knew we could handle him, but we didn't want to have to kill him.

So we took our foot in hand and started walking toward the water tanks. Major was happy to be out on the road. We followed the tracks out of town, and we said goodbye to some of the townspeople as we walked by. We were getting close to the water tanks when Major smelled a scent that he didn't recognize, so we slowed down and started being alert. We saw a group of saddled horses ground-hitched in some small trees away from the tracks. We were very careful not to be seen by the riders who were spread out along the tracks hidden from the bull and other railroad personnel. It looked to us that they were going to rob the train. It seemed we were not going to get on the train here, after all.

Will and I discussed the situation and decided that we should probably give the train crew a hand, if in fact this was a train robbery, and it sure looked like it was. We knew about what time the train would be getting to the water stop, so we had maybe fifteen minutes to get in an advantageous position ourselves so we could provide the best protection to the train and its passengers. We knew that this was a short train, not quite a bobtail. It had a passenger car, a livestock car, and express car, and we had been hoping for a couple of empty boxcars. We had our long guns, the rifles that we had purchased at the emporium fully loaded and ready for action. We waited there, hidden, for the action to unfold. We knew we had a humane and civic duty to perform, and we were determined to do our best.

We could hear the train coming up the ringing rails. The sound was getting louder and louder. We could hear the engine slowly getting ready to stop. The squeaking of the wheels as the brake was applied was ear-piercing, and then it shuttered in a cloud of steam to a stop. Out of the brush along the tracks came the train robbers, shooting and howling at the top of their lungs. The railroad bull came out of the caboose, and they shot him, and he fell to the ground. The robbers ran toward the express car, some to the passenger car, and some toward the engine trying to get the engineer under their control. Will and I opened up with our rifles, shooting the robbers, never missing a shot. We had no choice but to kill them as fast as we could. With our scathing fire, we soon stopped the raid and captured the remaining outlaws. Our practice on the irrigation canal paid off handsomely. This gang would not rob another train.

We placed the robbers—what was left of them—on the train, reversed the engines, and went back to Weiser, Idaho, where the sheriff took over and placed them under arrest and locked them up in a cell. The railroad bull was taken to the local doctor, and the report was that he would recover. The telegraph operator of the railroad sent the entire story over the wire to the home office. The citizens of Weiser, Idaho, and the customers in the passenger car hailed Will and me as heroes. We had saved the $58,000 payroll in the express car and saved the passengers' money and goods.

Jim Galloway came and said, "Bill, Will, you two are heroes," and told us he was glad of our good fortune. The hotel gave us free room and board for one week and free drinks at the bar. The bar owner knew he would do much more business because men wanted to congratulate me and Will's bravery and buy us drinks. Will and I sent a case of liquor to the hobo jungle. We told the mess moll to give it out sparingly. Three days after the robbery, a high-ranking official from the Old Great Northern Railroad came to Weiser upon the order of the president, James J. Hill. He rented a large dining room for an award ceremony for Will and me. All city dignitaries were invited as well as the common people; the room was overflowing. The railroad bull had recovered enough to come to the ceremony. The railroad dignitary furnished drinks on the house for the ceremony. The ceremony started quickly after Will and I and, of course, Major came into the room. Everyone stood up, clapping for the three. The railroad dignitary walked over to the podium and began.

He told how these two heroic men took on a gang of cutthroat train robbers all by ourselves to save the passengers' harm and money, how we fought the robbers to a standstill.

"They saved $58,000 in company payroll out of the bravery of their hearts."

He told the people how appreciative the owner and the stockholders of the Old Great Northern Railroad were to these brave men. He said that he had been authorized by the railroad to give lifetime passes on the Old Great Northern Railroad for free with all the amenities that these passes afforded and that he was also authorized to give them a check as a reward of 5 percent of the $58,000—or $2,900—reward.

The crowd went wild. They all rose to their feet, clapping their hands and enjoying the ceremony.

"Last but certainly not least," said the dignitary. "The sheriff has informed me there is a total of dead-or-alive reward on those bandits in the total sum of $2,500. You won't have to hobo anymore," he said.

We stayed in town for two more days after taking the reward money to the bank and depositing them under each name in the bank. We kept out $300 each for our trip to Fossil, Wheeler County, Oregon. We had decided, even though we now had the money, not to buy Wigwam or Papoose. It would now be easier and faster to travel on the train to our destination. At that point, we could decide where and what kind of horses, saddles, and tack that we wanted. Money changed everything, and we now had our small nest egg.

We arrived in Arlington, Oregon. It was the closest town with a train stop to Fossil, Oregon. At our first stop, we got a room at a run-down hotel, but it was supposedly the best that the city had to offer. We stowed our gear; took a bath to get the coal, smoke, and dust off our bodies; put on clean clothes; and went to find a livery stable.

On our way, we saw the sheriff's office and decided to call on him, let him know who we were, and ask a few questions. The sheriff was a little long in the tooth and had a robust stomach but seemed pleasant enough. We told him who we were and what our business was. We told him we were going to the café for something to eat and asked if he would care to join us. Looking at his stomach, I wasn't much surprised when he accepted our offer. During our lunch, we asked him if he knew the Double O Bar Ranch. He said he had heard of the ranch. It was a very large cattle ranch, and they ran about ten thousand steers, close to eight thousand mother cows and bulls. I told him that I was going to see my cousin, Robert Chestnut. He seemed to know my cousin, also as a top hand on the ranch. I asked him if there were anywhere in the immediate area that we could buy some good horse flesh.

He said, "There is an Indian reservation not too far away that sells Appaloosa horses," and he told us that we could probably find what we were looking for there. We thanked him and got directions to the reservation. I knew from talk and what I had read that Appaloosas were a fine breed of horses. Will had heard that also.

Next morning we went to the livery and asked the owner if he had any horses for sale or rent. He rented us horses for the time being to go to the Nez Perce Indian Reservation. Original Nez Perce tribes lived on the reservation in deep canyons along the Snake, Clearwater, and Salmon Rivers in Idaho; but this small group was a subtribe here in Eastern Oregon. They raised Appaloosas for sale. That's what we were looking for. The Appaloosa was bred with the rider in mind. He trained easily and was very intelligent you could guide him by the pressure of your knees without your hands on the bridle or the reins. In doing that, it left your hands free to rope or fight, whichever the case might be. The horse's hooves were very tough, and normally they didn't need horseshoes. All they needed was trimming periodically.

We were met at the gate of the reservation by two Indians riding on Appaloosa horses. They were absolutely beautiful specimens of the Appaloosa's bred. The Indians weren't hostile, but they did give a bearing of dignity and that they meant business. We told them that we were directed to come to the reservation inasmuch as we were looking for prime horse flesh, that the Nez Perce had the best stock in the vicinity. We were taken to the chief of this splintered tribe. He spoke English well and was the headman in all horse negotiations. We asked him if he had any horses for sale. We were looking for a pair, a stallion and a mare, so that we might start an Appaloosa herd far west of here. We would be of no competition to them.

The chief spoke in his own tongue to one of the braves—I assumed giving him orders to bring some horses for our viewing.

He offered us water, which we accepted out of politeness. If we had turned the water down, it would have been an affront to his dignity.

Two braves brought six animals—two stallions, two mares, and two gildings. They were beautiful horses, and Will and I stepped over to examine them. We started at the muzzle and rubbed our hands down the neck to the breasts, down each front leg, down his ribs and down the backbone to his hindquarters, and down each back leg. We checked their hooves and looked in their mouth at his teeth to tell age, and then Will jumped on one of the stallion's back and rode it in a circle until it was gasping for breath.

He stopped, jumped off, handed the reins to the spokesperson, and said, "This horse is wind-broken. I wouldn't buy this horse at any price. If this is all you have to offer, we appreciate your time, but we will move on and find some other animals. We don't need to look at your other animals."

"I have heard that Indians don't lie, this must be the exception to the rule," I said.

The chief stood up and said something to his braves in their own tongue. He then turned to Will and me and said, "Please forgive me and my braves for this deception. If you will allow me to show you two more horses, a stallion and a mare. I guarantee personally that they are sound, well-trained horses."

I said, "Okay, Chief, one more gamble, and we're gone."

He again spoke in his own tongue to the braves, and we sat there for ten minutes or so, and here came the brave leading two magnificent horses—a stallion and a mare. The only word that I can think of at the time was *magnificent*. The chief stood up, walked over to the reins of the two horses, brought them over to us, and pressed the reins into our hands.

He said, "These are two of our finest, you be the judge."

After the last debacle, we examined these two horses from top to bottom. We found them in perfect physical condition and after riding them knew that these two horses where the cream of their crop.

We sat there with the chief, saying nothing, just looking at him, saying with our eyes that we understood. After five minutes or so, he spoke to us first in his native language and second in English.

He said, "I humbly apologize for trying to sell you inferior mounts. I want to make up for shaming my Indian brothers for telling you that lie. You understand our customs well. So I am offering you these two prize animals at this ridiculously low price. You can have each of these animals for $100, and along with the horses is my sincere apology."

Will and I knew that these were superior mounts. We knew that the price that he quoted us was a steal, and we knew that nowhere could we find horses of this quality.

I said, "Chief, you do us honor by presenting these horses to us at this price. We will accept these beautiful animals from you, but not at a $100 each. But we will give you $300 for both and accept your heartfelt apology. You can be sure that we will care for these animals as well as you have cared for them."

We placed a lead rope on the two horses and headed back to the livery stable and Arlington. We were two days from town getting supper when three riders rode up to our camp. Major heard them coming and alerted us. They rode in like it was their camp. Automatically, we became suspicious of them. In the West, you always hello the camp and asked for permission to ride into someone's camp, but not these yeah-whos. They walked over to our horses and got a good look at them.

They said, "Fine horse flesh."

Will said, "We agree on that." Will said, "We just bought them from the Nez Perce Indians today."

The man said, "Must have cost a tidy sum."

Will said, "Some."

The man's hand was going to his gun butt, and I knew he was going to draw. I reached behind my neck and threw the knife at his throat, hitting him squarely. Both of his hands flew to his throat, but it was too late, and he was too weak to pull out the knife. He toppled over on the ground. Will shot one man, and we doubled on the last man.

Will said, "You're hell on wheels with those knives, Bill."

And I said, "Some."

We pulled the bandits away from camp for the night and continued our supper. Next morning we threw the bodies across their saddles, tied them down, put a lead rope on their horses also—we had quite a caravan—and headed for the sheriff's office in Arlington.

It was dark when we reached the sheriff's office. We wanted to push on and not have to spend another night on the trail with three dead bodies, and I knew that they were beginning to stink. We rode up to the sheriff's office, but he was not there. He had his night deputy covering for him as he had gone home to his wife. We told the deputy our story and that we were going to take our horses to the livery stable return the mounts that we had rented and if he would contact the undertaker to come get these bodies. He said that he would do all that. We went to the hotel's restaurant and got a late supper and went to bed, waiting for the morning to come and our explanation to the sheriff.

The next morning we were awakened by a loud pounding on the door. Will went to the door and let the sheriff in the room.

"I'm sorry, boys, but I couldn't let you sleep any longer. Those three were wanted dead or alive, you boys did a good thing. There's a reward of $1,000 on the three. You boys can pick it up at my office this afternoon after I go to the bank."

"Thank you, Sheriff," I said.

"It seems we are bounty hunters now. We left all their gear with the livery hand, you can give those ponies and all their gear over to the town coffers or use them as you see fit," said Will.

We told the deputy our story.

"Sheriff, do you need anything else? With your permission, we will leave Arlington tomorrow for Fossil, Oregon, and then on to the Double O Bar Ranch."

The sheriff said, "I have no reason to hold either of you, so you're free to go."

After breakfast, we went over to the saddle shop to look at saddles for each of us and get additional gear that we needed for our new Appaloosas. I chose a beautiful saddle that was hand-tooled with flowers on the inside and outside of the cantle with a basket weave on the back of the cantle. It had double girths, and it was made by the famous saddlemaker from Weiser, Idaho, shipped to Arlington for resale. Will chose an equally beautiful saddle for his horse. We also chose our bridles with snaffle bits and extra-long reins. The saddle blankets were handwoven by the Indians and were very easy on the horses' back and beautifully colored. We bought two lariats and a rifle scabbard for each saddle.

As it was a two-day ride to Fossil, and another seventy miles to the Double O Bar Ranch, we decided we had better buy some trail gear and grub so we would be comfortable along the way. We also bought two medium-sized canteens because we didn't know the water situation ahead. We had our handguns. Will had his .38 pistol, and I had the .45 that I had gotten from Jim Galloway. I paid him for that weapon before we left, so I guess we were loaded for bear and hope we didn't meet one. These horses that we had bought—and got a bill of sale for, by the way—were the cream of the crop. Will said that he had never ridden a horse this good, and being not as good a horseman and expert as Will, I had to agree. We had bought a pack mule for our goods so we would not burden our riding horses. We were on our way.

I was sure most of us could remember back when we were fifteen to sixteen years old and some of the events that happened then that shaped our lives. But when I started to remember, I got a little melancholy—remembering my dad and the farm and the not-long-enough time that I had to spend with him. I remembered being thrown off the farm by my stepmother, remembered when Dad and I went and bought Major. I remember hopping a train like a hobo; remember the job on the canal with Mr. Calloway and Will; remember the snakebite and the death of Ray; remember the fight with the train robbers; remember the buying of our horses; remember the bandits who tried to steal our horses and kill us; remember the Nez Perce Indians, their lies and apologies; the killing of the three men and the bounty that we collected on them and the train robbers. Looking back on it, it seemed surreal, like this had happened to someone else and I was just a bystander looking on. I couldn't believe that Will and I had gained a reputation as gunfighters and bounty hunters. I was only a little over sixteen years old. The first night was uneventful, just another night under the stars. We did have our duties to our stock. I learned that Will was a passable cook and coffee maker. We left at first dawn. I was getting used to my mare. She was very well trained, and it was a pleasure to ride her. I believed she was part thoroughbred from her look. And I believed she was as fast as Will's stallion—if not faster. I knew she would be a terrific brood mare, which was my ultimate intent.

We were on our last leg of our journey to the ranch when I heard a woman screaming and the sound of a fast-running horse. I dropped the lead rope on the pack mule and started toward the noise. I saw a woman on a black horse that was out of control. She was doing her best to stop the animal, but she was having no luck. I reined my horse in her direction and put on the speed that I knew the mare was capable of. The woman saw me coming, but she still couldn't stop the horse. I was gaining fast. I had never turned my mare loose at top speed before. She was magnificent. My horse was eating up the distance between the two horses rapidly. I could tell she was a good horsewoman, as she had grown up on a ranch, but there was not much anyone could do. If the horse got the bit in his teeth, and bit down on the bit, a person couldn't guide or stop the horse. I knew because it had happened to me. A woman didn't have the strength to get a bit out of the horse's teeth. Quickly thinking, I decided to take the woman off her saddle, which would be safer. Here was where I would use my knees to guide the mare and use her training. I would be able to use both hands, grabbing the woman off her saddle. My mare performed beautifully, feeling my every move, compensating for it. As I came along beside the horse, I hollered for her to kick out of the stirrups and I would pick her off the saddle. Everything went smoothly, and the mare came to a slow stop, not a sudden stop. She knew what was best for her riders. I helped the woman off my horse. She was a little shaken up but not unduly so. She was a woman of the ranch.

To my surprise, she wasn't a woman after all. She was a young girl about my age and very pretty, and that was good. She had light-red hair and blue-green-emerald-colored eyes.

She said, "I am very grateful for your rescue. I could have been hurt gravely. My name is Patricia O'Brien, and my father owns the Double O Bar."

"This is a coincidence, since we were heading for the Double O Bar," I said. "My cousin, Robert Chestnut, is supposed to work there. My name is William Chestnut. Most folks call me Bill, and I was going there to look him up. I haven't seen Robert since I was a young boy. But we always got along."

Patricia said, "I should've known, you are a gentleman and a good rider like your cousin Bobby."

"Yes, ma'am," I said. "We have heard back in our hometown that Bobby is a top hand."

About that time, Will rode up with Patricia's black horse, which he had caught up. I introduced Will to Patricia O'Brien and told him she was the daughter of the owner of the Double O Bar Ranch.

Will tipped his hat and said, "Mighty glad to meet you, ma'am. I caught up your horse for you. Hope you didn't get hurt."

"No," said Patricia, "Bill saved me from injury, and thank you for bringing up my horse. Would you two like to ride back to the ranch with me?"

"Yes, ma'am," we said in unison, "it would be a pleasure."

We talked in small talk until we got in sight of the ranch. Will and I both stopped and looked at the beautiful ranch lying in the valley before us. It was a picture like you would see in a New York magazine—beautiful green grass, white fences, snowcapped mountains in the background. I could see white-faced Herford cattle in some pens close to what I believed to be the bunkhouse. And some cowboys were walking around, but they were too far away to be recognizable.

Patricia said, "I want you to come up to the ranch house with me. I want to introduce you to my father and mother," as we rode through the large wrought iron decorated gate. It had wrought-iron cutouts of horses and cattle along the top of the gate, simply beautiful.

As we rode along, Patricia said, "You two have the most beautiful animals I have ever seen."

We told her about our episode with the Nez Perce Indians and how we came to own them. She thought that was a delightful, exciting experience.

When we rode up to the large ranch house, two cowboys hurriedly came over and took the reins of our mounts and said, "We'll take care of your animals while you're here."

We dismounted and walked with Patricia up on the porch.

She hollered, "Mom, Dad, I have someone I want you to meet."

When her mother and dad came through the front door onto the porch, they stopped and looked at us but said nothing. He was a handsome man and his wife, Patricia's mother, was a beautiful woman.

Patricia said, "Mom, Dad, this is William Chestnut, Robert's first cousin, who has come to see his relative, and this is Williams's friend, Will."

Will and I tipped our hats and said, "Happy to meet you and your wife."

Patricia continued saying, "Blackie got the bit in his teeth and started running, and I couldn't stop him. A bobcat jumped out of the brush in front of Blackie, and he bolted. William saw my urgent predicament and came after me on his magnificent Appaloosa mare. He saved me from serious injury, riding alongside and picking me out of the saddle before I could be seriously hurt. Will caught up with Blackie and brought him back to us."

Patricia's mother came over and hugged her daughter and shook our hands, saying, "Thank you so much for your help."

Patricia's father came over and shook our hands and said, "Thank you so much. My name is Thomas O'Brien, at your service. Call me Tom."

"Mom, Dad," said Patricia, "could we invite Bill, Bobby, and Will to have dinner with us tonight? That's the least I can do."

"I can certainly do that, Patricia, and it's a small thing for what they did for you and us today," Mr. O'Brien said. "Men, let's sit over there on the porch at the table and have some refreshments."

Patricia's mother went in the house and came back with a large pitcher of lemonade with ice. I was certainly surprised about the ice, and I asked Mr. O'Brien where he had gotten it.

He said, "Up in the mountains, there are some volcanic tunnels, and inside those tunnels are ice the year round. We call them the ice caves, some of my punchers take a wagon up there and chip out the ice and bring it down to the ranch, and we pack it in sawdust so we have ice almost all year round. Now, I want to hear your stories, please tell me."

I said, "There's not too much to tell about me, Mr. O'Brien. My mother, whom I never met, died at childbirth. Dad remarried, and my stepmother, I believe, resented me. She didn't harm me in any way, but she didn't help Dad raise me a whole lot either. When Dad died almost a year ago, she asked me to leave the farm. I was about sixteen and a half years old but was good-size boy for my age. I didn't have much time to debate what I should do, so I did as my dad said he had done when he was young. I hopped on a freight train and started hoboing going West. I got off the train ahead of the train guard—or bull, as they are called—in Weiser, Idaho, and went to the hobo jungle where I met up with Will, and we got a job working on the irrigation canal out of Weiser. The owner of the canal is Jim Galloway, and a nice man. We told Mr. Galloway that we were going to find my cousin, Robert Chestnut, who works on a ranch in Oregon. When the weather cools down and he didn't need us on the canal for the winter, we had no thought of making the canal work a permanent vocation. We appreciate Mr. Galloway's help getting us on our feet and on the ground, giving us an opportunity to later make our own way. Sometime, if you or your family really want to know the details of that employment, Will and I will be happy to tell you."

"We didn't have enough money saved out of our wages to pay the railroad fare or to buy horses and equipment to continue our journey to find Robert, so we decided to take the risk and the wrath of the railroad bull and hobo again to Eastern Oregon," I said. "We talked to the other hobos and found that the train to catch was the Old Great Northern Railroad and that it stopped on the other side of the town to take on water, and we decided to board there. In walking the three miles from the outskirts of town to the water tanks, my dog, Major, with his actions told us that there were men up ahead. We saw some ground-hitched horses and riders along the track, which gave us an idea what they planned to do—rob the train.

"We decided that it is our duty to help the train people and its passengers, so we hid ourselves in the brush. The train came and stopped at the water towers to take on water, and then the robbers attacked. Will and I went into action and stopped the robbery and captured what was left of them. We took them back to Weiser and turned them over to the sheriff. The town and the passengers congratulated us and gave us a week's stay rent-free and board-free at the local hotel. The Old Northern Railroad sent a dignitary to Weiser to congratulate us on saving the train and its passengers, along with saving the $58,000 payroll that was in the baggage car. They also gave free lifetime passes on the railroad, along with all of the amenities that a lifetime pass affords. They also gave us a check for 5 percent of the payroll that we saved, or $2,900. The sheriff of the town presented us with a check for $2,000, which was a dead-or-alive reward for the robbers. I don't want to bore you with more of our escapades. We went and bought two Appaloosa horses from the Nez Perce Indians and the gear to continue our trip to locate Bobby."

Patricia's mother said, "Quite an extraordinary, exciting young life you've had so far. It is no wonder that you are a fine, upstanding gentleman. You're welcome here."

Mr. O'Brien stood up from the table walked around the table to me and said, "Welcome," also to Will. That was all he needed to say; I knew he meant it, at that time.

Mr. O'Brien said, "Boys, go on down to the bunkhouse and pick out a bunk. We'll talk again after Bobby gets here and we have our supper tonight."

"Yes, sir," we said.

We got up, left the porch, and walked toward the bunkhouse. Our horses were tied to the hitch rail out front; the girths had been loosened; and it looked like one of the men had curried down the animals as much as he could without removing the saddles. We removed our bedrolls and rifles and carried them inside the bunkhouse. A couple of cowboys were in the bunkhouse, and we asked them which bunks were available, and they showed us a couple against the north wall. They were fine with us. We introduced ourselves, saying that we were friends of Bobby Chestnut and probably would only stay here for a couple of days. We took our animals to the barn to find two stalls, for the Appaloosas and one for our pack mule. We removed the saddles and the gear, carried them down, watered, and fed the animals. The cowboys at the bunkhouse immediately recognized that Will was one of them. He was a "cowboy." I, on the other hand, was a question mark.

We unrolled our bedrolls, got out our best Sunday go-to meeting clothes, tried to straighten out the wrinkles, and got ready for the supper engagement with Bobby and the O'Brien family. We asked the cowboys where we could find a tub of water to wash the grime off, and they pointed out back to the horse trough. We accepted their invitation and did the best we could under the circumstances. We also shaved. I didn't need to shave much.

I asked Will if he had any polish or anything that could make my boots shine. I wanted to look good for Patricia and her mother.

He said, "I have some bear grease that I used on my saddle before I had to sell it. If you want to use that, you're welcome."

It was about five thirty in the afternoon when the cowboys started drifting back to the bunkhouse after doing the job assignment that had been given them in the morning. As they came in, Will and I introduced ourselves. When Bobby came in, he had a private room in the back of the bunkhouse, which was his quarters, and he ran the ranch from there. He never even looked in our direction, and to tell the truth, I barely recognized him. Of course, he was older than when I saw him last, and I was a lot younger then. But he had filled out and made a handsome cowboy. There was an Indian with him, and they went into the office together. One of the cowboys said that the Indian was Bobby's competition in the Pendleton Roundup rodeo, but because he as an Indian, he didn't get a lot of recognition. His American name was Jack Sundown, but his Indian name was Waaya Tonch Toiesib Kahn, and he had quite a history behind him.

He was born in 1866. He was a full Lakota Sioux, and after the battle of the Little Bighorn and the killing of Custer, Jack Sundown went to Canada with Chief Sitting Bull in 1877. He was eleven years old. He came back with Chief Sitting Bull to the Indian reservation at Standing Rock. All this happened before Chief Sitting Bull joined up with Buffalo Bill Cody's Wild West show. I didn't know if Jack Sundown had any influence on Sitting Bull's decision to join Buffalo Bill show. But I did know Bobby and Jack; they stuck together like glue. About an hour until suppertime, a middle-aged lady came down to the bunkhouse and told Bobby that he should come to the main house for supper tonight and that Mr. O'Brien had something to discuss with him, and of course, he said he would. I assumed that she would ask Will and me to come to supper also, but we already had an invitation and weren't given another. We already did all the cleaning up we could, anyway, so we just waited until Bobby came out of his private bunkhouse room, and we sort of sauntered along behind him.

He turned around and said, "Who are you, men?"

We said, "We're two strangers here on the ranch, and we have been invited up to supper."

As we got close to the front door, it opened, and Patricia came out dressed to the nines. She was simply beautiful.

She said, "Bobby, men, Daddy is waiting for you in the sitting room, and supper will be ready shortly."

As we went to the sitting room, Mr. O'Brien said, "Welcome, come in, gentlemen, have a seat, supper will be ready shortly." Mr. O'Brien said, "Bobby, you are the best foreman that a rancher could ask for. I have never interfered with your hiring and your firing methods on this ranch. You are still the foreman and the top hand, I don't want to usurp your authority in this case, but I would like for you, if you see fit, to hire these two gentlemen. One of them is your first cousin from your hometown, the younger one, William Chestnut. The other one is his friend Will."

Bobby jumped up and came over to me, grabbed me by the shoulders, and hugged me tightly as he said, "I knew there was something familiar about you. What are you doing here?"

"It's a long story, Bobby, and some rainy day I'll tell you the entire story. But now I'm just glad to see you and renew our friendship. I didn't come here to ask for a job because I'm no cowboy, but I wouldn't refuse one if offered. I know Will would be very grateful, but he can speak for himself. I believe he is a good cowboy and has been a loyal friend to me."

Bobby said, "Okay, boys. You are hired, your pay is a dollar a day and found, starting today."

I said, "Bobby, I'm not a cowboy. I don't deserve a dollar a day, but I will work hard to earn the name cowboy!"

Patricia walked into the room and said, "Supper is served."

At the supper table, Patricia told her side of the story—of my rescuing her, about Blackie, about the bobcat, about their magnificent Appaloosas. Bobby's ears perked up as he listened to the praise of his first cousin. He knew by what he had just heard that I had the makings of a top hand. He didn't know about my shooting ability or his prowess with the knives; that would come later. After supper, the men retired to the study, where Mr. O'Brien offered a glass of brandy and a cigar to us.

I told him, "Thanks, anyway, but I don't drink or smoke."

He had Patricia bring out a pot of coffee and a couple of cups, and of course, I was always happy to look at Patricia. After a little small talk, Bobby suggested that we had better go to the bunkhouse and get some sleep.

"Mornings come early on a cattle ranch, and you usually worked till sundown."

We said our thanks to Mr. and Mrs. O'Brien and to Patricia and told them to give our congratulations to the cook for a wonderful meal and went along with Bobby to the bunkhouse. Bobby was still asking me questions as I got in to my bunk.

I said, "We had better sleep now, Bobby, we'll talk as long as you want in the morning. I'm sure worn out."

Next morning we were introduced to all the cowboys, and they were told that we were members of the crew. We expected to hold our own end of the work log as they did. Bobby wanted me to work with Jack Sundown. He was a top cowboy, and Bobby felt that I could learn faster with him. I accepted that assignment gratefully, for I knew that Jack and Bobby were friends and Jack would do his best to teach a novice the way of the "cowboy," which I was eager to learn. Jack made a comment that my Appaloosa looked to be an exceptionally fine animal. I shook my head yes and said so. In riding alongside Jack, he told me that Bobby was worried about rustlers in the area.

"They have been helping themselves to our beef. And he has vowed to stop it, our brand is not too easy to change with a running iron, it would take an artist, and there were plenty to choose from in the rustler's trade."

I was working with Jack, and he was teaching me the art of being a cowboy as fast as I could learn. He was an excellent teacher, but maybe I was a slow learner. He hadn't said so. We were riding along at the end of the day heading back to the bunkhouse when we scared two coyotes out of the brush.

Jack hollered, "Shoot them, Bill," and I drew and fired, killing both coyotes quick as a wink.

Jack had stopped his horse and was sitting there, looking at me, as if he had never seen me before or if I had horns.

He said, "Bill, where did you ever learn to shoot like that?"

I said, "When Will and I was working on the irrigation canal and we were in Idaho, Will and I had lots of practice. Will is as good a shot with his .38 as I am with my .45, we don't miss."

"Remarkable," said Jack. "Wait till Bobby hears about this."

Ever since Bobby had been involved in the local rodeos, the ranch hands put aside their daily jobs every three months on Sunday morning to have a miniature ranch rodeo. Some of the cow hands wanted to show off their skills at horseback riding, bareback riding, and bull riding. They also wanted to show their skills at shooting, so next Sunday morning was the day that all this was going to happen. The owners of the ranch, the O'Briens, were always part of the audience and always gave the winning cowboy a small bonus. There were a few bleacher seats, which we all occupied. Most all of the cowboys participated in the events, but you could see quickly that Bobby and Jack Sundown were going to be the overall winners. Both were excellent riders. At the end of the riding events, you could say that it was a tied event, so the O'Briens gave both Bobby and Jack a small bonus. Then came the shooting event, and we all moved further out into the pasture so that no one would be in danger of being hurt during the competition. The first competition was with the long guns. Each cowboy took his turn at the target two hundred yards away. If you were successful in hitting the first target, you would try the second target three hundred yards away; that was nine hundred feet and would be one hell of a shot. No one had so far hit the three hundred-yard target, and Will and I—being the most recent addition to the crew—were last. I had my Henry and Will his 3006. Both of us hit the target with the first shot. The cowboys picked up the three hundred-foot yard target and moved it back to four hundred yards. Will and I fired an again both hit the target. Again the cowboys moved the target to five hundred yards; this was almost getting ridiculous. We both fired at the target, and we both missed. It was called a draw. We were awarded our small bonuses, as if each of us had won.

It was the time for the pistol competition. The targets were set much closer, and the targets were shaped like a wagon wheel with six protruding spokes. Each cowboy was to draw and fire and hit as many of the protrusions as possible. Each of the cowboys took their turn, but none hit all six protrusions—not even Bobby or Jack hit all six. Again, as the last two members of the crew and low on the totem pole, it was our turn. Will took the first attempt; he hit five protrusions. Now was my turn, and I was hoping I wouldn't mess up because Patricia was looking, and I wanted her to be impressed by my shooting. I told a cowboy to go and turn the wheel until it coasted. When he had done that, I pulled my pistol fast and fanned the hammer, holding down the trigger, and hit all six protrusions before the wheel stopped. There was silence.

No one made any noise. They were dumbfounded, and then a thunderous roar and clapping and whistling from the audience—they had never seen a cowboy shoot like that.

Patricia came up and said to me, "That was a remarkable exhibition of shooting skills, you sure have earned this bonus today."

The other cowboys—including Bobby and Jack—came over, shook my hand, and patted my back.

Bobby said, "Extraordinary."

That was all he needed to say.

After the rodeo was over, O'Brien said, "We have prepared a special dinner for you men, and the cook has made some bear sign for your dessert." (They are homemade donuts.) "If you have ever seen bear sign, or scat, you would know why they are called that."

The supper and the rodeo was a tremendous success.

The next day after our assignments was given to us. I asked Bobby about the rustlers. He told me that the ranch has lost anywhere from fifty to seventy steers so far this year, unaccounted for, and he had seen hoof prints that he decided did not belong to the crew on the ranch, so they must be the prints of the rustlers' horses.

I asked him when the last time was that he had seen these prints.

He said, "A week or ten days ago. It looked as if they were driving ten or so steers, and we followed them as far as we could, and then we lost the tracks in the rocks and brush."

I said, "Next time, Bobby, you see horse tracks, can Will and I follow them, along with Major? Major has a good nose. He's no bloodhound, but he can follow scent, and I would like, along with Will and Major, to find the stolen cattle for the ranch. You know that Will and I can take care of ourselves. They must be holding the cattle somewhere in the Badlands for the changed brands to heal. You know, there are Badlands in Oregon as well as the Badlands of South Dakota. It will be interesting to see whose brand the rustlers put on the steers with their running iron. During the days that followed, several ranchers in the greater vicinity came over to the Double O Bar to talk about the rustlers. This rustling was certainly getting out of hand, and it must be stopped."

A week later, Bobby came into the bunkhouse and said, "It's happened again, we have lost steers, the rustlers are on the move, and I've lost the trail."

I said, "Okay, Will and I and Major will pick up where you left off. Where is it?"

He told us the general location where he had lost the tracks, and we went to the cookhouse and got some provisions to last a few days.

On our way back from the cook shack, we ran into Jack Sundown, who said he wanted to go with us to find those rustlers.

I said, "Jack, there's no one I would rather have along better than you, let's get cracking."

Bobby took us to the location where he had lost the trail. Jack, Will, Major, and I looked over the area. We too saw where the trail and the cattle had disappeared. We looked at Jack.

He said, "I believe this was done yesterday afternoon. There should be a good scent lingering in the area on the grass."

I got down off my horse, took Major by the collar, walked him over to where we saw the last of the cattle trail, and I told him to fetch. I had taught Major to fetch when he was a young pup, and he knew very well what it meant. He put his nose to the ground and smelled for scent. I could tell that he had picked up the scent of the cattle and perhaps the outlaws. The four of us, including Major, knew this was not going to be an easy task that we had set for ourselves, but we were determined to ride out our string until we found the outlaws. Major, with the short legs, was easy to follow, and he knew we were close behind him, so he didn't bark on the trail. We were trying to keep as quite as possible and not alert the outlaws. We were traveling at twice the speed of a herd of cattle that was driven by cowboys, so each day we were gaining on the rustlers.

The third day out, we could hear some cattle bawling up ahead. We decided that Jack was better equipped with his Indian blood and training to sneak up on the outlaws' camp and reconnoiter the circumstances and report back.

We stepped off our horses, and I said, "We will wait for Jack to get back and make our plans then."

Jack returned in about two hours, telling us that he had located the cattle. They were in a box canyon, and they had a natural water supply from a small creek running out of the mountains, and there were four men guarding them. He said that, to his surprise, he recognized one of the men that was in our own Double O Bar crew. He was a traitor to his brand. We talked about different means of capturing these outlaw rustlers but could not come to any solution other than meet them head-on. We should take time with cool heads to devise a plan that would be successful with no injuries if possible to our crew. I told Jack and Will that we should try and capture one alive, that the owners of the ranches involved could question in detail. With that in mind, we devised a plan that would put each of us on three different sides and waited until dark. After they had their supper, we would attack them then. We didn't want to kill them, but we could take no chances with any of our lives. Jack could mimic the sound of a whip-poor-will—which was a night bird, almost undetectable, as a false bird. We would all try to be in place, and when Jack gave the sound of the whip-poor-will, then all three would attack. We had a couple of hours to sneak up on camp quietly without them seeing or hearing us. It was my job to keep Major quite.

All was in readiness. The three of us stepped out into the fire-light of their camp.

Each fired our weapons in the air, and we hollered, "Drop your guns."

They didn't, and we opened a devastating fire with our weapons. Three men fell quickly. One ducked behind a rock, but he didn't know that Jack was there, waiting for him. Jack hit him with the barrel of his rifle, knocking him unconscious. We had three outlaws dead and one captured, who happened to be one of the Double O Bars former crew members. We tied him securely, ate some jerky, made some coffee, and waited the night out. Our planning ahead made the exercise workable and the injuries down to zero on our side.

As false dawn approached, we gathered up the outlaws' horses, tied their bodies across the saddles, threw the outlaw who had regained consciousness on his horse and laced him securely, and rounded up the cattle. We assumed it to be a few over one hundred head, but with three men pushing them hard, we were sure we could get them back to the Double O Bar in two days. We didn't treat the traitor roughly, but we didn't give him any slack either. He's the kind of cowboy that gives "cowboys" a bad name. As we approached our home headquarters, we saw lights from lanterns being lit like fire-flies in the night. They, evidently, could hear the hundred plus cattle bawling at the ranch, and we saw cowboys run to the corrals opening up the gates to let the herd in.

We saw the O'Briens coming out of the ranch house and onto the porch, and we saw Bobby and our ranch hands coming toward us. I saw Patricia coming down the steps of the porch, running toward the corral. I was hoping that she was running to see me. But I didn't know for sure. I saw Bobby with his rifle in his hand, and some of the other crew had their weapons as well, as they didn't know what was happening for sure, but they could not take any undue chances. The men were shouting and calling out our names; we were a motley-looking crew. Some of the cowboys grabbed the reins of the traitor's horse and took him over to the hitch rail. I handed Bobby the running iron that Henry had in his saddlebags, which was normally enough to get your neck stretched on the spot. Mr. O'Brien and his wife were standing on the edge of the porch and were joining in the excitement of the returning of the cattle.

We stepped down off of our horses, and everyone gathered around to ask questions, so fast that we couldn't answer.

I said, "Patricia, I'm sorry, I look so bad, we didn't have time to clean up."

She said, "Bill, you look marvelous to me."

I believed Patricia's mother heard that remark. She asked me if we had anything to eat most of the day, and we said no; we were too anxious to get the herd back to our home corral. The O'Briens told us to come into the house. They would have the cook fix us something to eat, and we could wash up on the back porch, and then after we were cleaned up and satisfied with our delayed supper, we could tell them our story, in every small detail. Mr. O'Brien told Bobby to send one of the cowboys to all the ranches involved and to bring back one of the cowboys with each of them to drive their rescued cattle back to their ranges.

He also told Bobby to send for the sheriff.

Bobby said, "Mr. O'Brien, I don't think that's the right thing to do at this time. I may be completely wrong, and I hope I am, but Henry may be in cahoots with the sheriff. I saw them together last time I was in town, and they looked cozy to me. I couldn't hear them, which put me thinking, and I want you and the other ranchers to question Henry before we decide what's proper for him."

Mr. O'Brien said, "I would never have thought the sheriff was in on the rustling that's going on."

I could hear some of the ranch hands saying, "We ought to hang the son of a bitch."

I didn't want that kind of talk to get started and told them so. We posted a guard on Henry's place of confinement. It was just a fortified storage room; we didn't want to take any chances. If he attempted to escape, shoot to kill.

The other ranchers that were affected by the rustlers soon started drifting in to the Double O Bar. They had a million questions, but Mr. O'Brien hesitated to say very much until all the ranchers were present.

When all the ranchers were there, Mr. O'Brien took them all into this study along with Bobby. Will, Jack, and I decided we had no ax to grind and any decision made should be made by the owners that were harmed by the rustlers. Mr. O'Brien and Bobby knew of our participation in finding the cattle and bringing them back to our ranch so they could answer most any questions that the other ranchers might have, but we kept ourselves available, just in case we were called to clear up a point.

The discussion with the ranchers went on for several hours, and then Mr. O'Brien came out and said, "Bobby, go get Henry, and bring him here, some of the ranchers need answers to their questions. Out of the three rustlers that we had killed, two of them belonged to the ranchers in the room."

Out came Henry. He still had his hands tied, and he was pale as a ghost. We were sure he had been reliving what the punishment could be, and in those days hanging was justified. Jack, Will, and I stayed away from the meeting but would be around if needed. Time passed slowly as the hands on the ranch and we three waited on the decision of the ranchers.

Henry talked freely under the threat of hanging and told the ranchers what he knew. He told them that he didn't know who the main boss was but that the sheriff was a liaison to the boss and the rustlers and that if we wanted to know more, we would have to talk to the sheriff. By now it was getting late and the ranchers all decided to meet in town tomorrow morning. Even the ranchers that had not been a victim were to be notified of the meeting and all would be present. They and their cowboys herded their steers back to their home range but would be ready for the meeting two days in town at the Granger Hall. Bobby said that Mr. O'Brien would like Jack, Will, and me to be at the meeting and that we could all ride together. It was a two-day ride. We would hold Henry outside of town until we were told to bring him on in. They wanted to go in and disarm the sheriff, lock him up in his own jail, and then confront him with Henry and Henry's story. This plan was carried out with no fanfare, and we were told to bring Henry to the jail. All the ranchers in the greater vicinity were waiting for Henry to show. The ranchers had gotten the mayor of Fossil, the town council, and all were present.

When confronting the sheriff with Henry and his testimony, the sheriff reluctantly admitted his duplicity. He was relieved of his badge and put in the cell next to Henry to await the circuit judge and their trial. The sheriff would not tell who the big boss was, but we figured that upon threat of hanging from the judge, he would spill his guts. As several of us knew, he was a coward.

Anyway, I had no idea when I went to the Double O Bar ranch that I would meet up with someone from my hometown besides Bobby. He was a fugitive from the law because he had shot and killed a preacher by the name of Walker, off his mule, coming back from church. The two families were feuding. There was a warrant out for his arrest, so he skipped town, and no one knew where he had gone until I ran across him here at the ranch. He asked me to promise that I would tell no one of his whereabouts, but when we went into town, he would ride his horse up and down the Main Street of Fossil, shooting his .38 special up in the air and daring the sheriff, who was looking out the saloon window, to come out and fight. I could tell other stories about the cowboy from my hometown, but not at this moment; this wasn't the time. The sheriff had let the corrupt head of greed outweigh his common sense. And if you danced to the rustlers' devil music, you must pay the fiddler—one way or the other.

The ranchers met with the mayor and the council people to discuss whom they could hire as a sheriff pro tem until a new election could be held. At that meeting, they also decided to give as a reward to Jack, Will, and myself a sum of $100 each. We had not looked or thought of a reward when we were in the Badlands trying to capture the rustlers, but it was a welcome gesture. So I guess now Will and I were—supposedly—gunmen, bounty hunters, and range detectives. And I was only seventeen and a half years old.

With all the excitement, we were becoming passé. We settled back to the running of the Double O Bar ranch. That was until we heard that the circuit judge would be in Fossil in two weeks for the trials of the sheriff and Henry. The council and the mayor wanted Will to become sheriff pro tem, but he said he was a cowboy and that was all he wanted to be—other than being my friend, which touched my heart. Since the first meeting at the hobo jungle, Will and I had become very close friends. He was older than I was, but that didn't seem to matter. We respected each other's feelings.

One of the town's councilmen of Fossil, Oregon, became sheriff pro tem. He was just a figurehead and did the administrative work, but he was instructed to keep down the names and addresses of any visitors that wanted to speak to the sheriff or Henry. They felt that it was important to know who the visitors were. The judge came and set a date for the trial, one week from his arrival. The trial would be held in the Fossil courthouse. The high feelings against the prisoners were somehow relaxed due to the passing of time, but the interest was still prominent. The prisoners had been relaxed, hoping for someone to help them; but now, since the circuit judge had arrived, they were worried. The local frenzy had stepped up the prisoners anxiously. The prisoners had hopes that the big shots and bosses would help them in some way to beat this rap and get them out of jail. But it was becoming plain that they could do very little. A dark night, when there was no moon, some men—we don't know who yet—came to the jail, shot the sheriff pro tem, and also killed both prisoners so they couldn't name the brain behind the rustlers. They had just paid the fiddler, I guess it was better than being hanged, but it had the same deadly conclusion.

Winter came to Eastern Oregon. Just because it got cold didn't diminish our cowboying duties on the ranch. There wasn't much natural graze on the high land, so the cowboys had to move their herds to the lowlands and supplement their grass with hay. They had to cut it by hand. It was an arduous task. It was also a time when the cowboys could practice their expertise on the contest that they were going to enter in the Pendleton Roundup rodeo. Jack had heard by the grapevine that Sitting Bull had been granted leave from the Standing Rock Reservation and was going to star, along with some of his braves, in the Buffalo Bill Wild West show and that he would like to come by the Double O Bar ranch and see his good friend Jack Sundown. Many of the ranch hands had heard about Jack's relationship with Sitting Bull, but a lot of them didn't believe it. Now was a chance for them to eat crow. As anyone could imagine, it was an exciting time on the ranch. The architect and the general of the battle at greasy grass, or the Battle of Little Big Horn, and the killing of Colonel Armstrong Custer and his troopers were fresh in the public's mind. It had been rumored that Chief Crazy Horse was the one that actually killed Custer.

Tom O'Brien and his family were willing hosts to a large party to be given at the ranch, and other ranchers and their hands were also invited. We were instructed to pick out two steers, bring them into the corrals, and feed them grain for a few months to fatten them for the gala party—which Mr. O'Brien wanted to throw for Chief Sitting Bull and his braves (and also his squaws, we can't forget them). There was going to be a mini rodeo on the ranch so that each ranch participant could hone his or her skills for the Pendleton Roundup and also for the pleasure of Setting Bull. Mr. O'Brien put Jack Sundance in charge to see that everything went well. All was in readiness when the mayor of Fossil, Oregon, rode out to the ranch—which was seventy miles from town—and he was a little tired and weary from the trip but excited. His news was that Buffalo Bill Cody had heard that Sitting Bull had accepted his offer to come to the Wild West show, so he wanted to come to the Double O Bar and extend to Sitting Bull his ceremonial welcome to the show. Can you imagine the excitement that this news brought to the ranch? Two very famous people at the same time would be Double O Bars guests—William Frederick

Cody and visionary holy war Indian Chief Sitting Bull? What a hand to draw to! Cody's entourage was added to the guest list.

Mr. O'Brien said, "Add another steer to the corral, the party is getting larger."

The word was spreading like wildfire on dry Buffalo grass. The Double O Bar was having famous dignitaries at their party. It was going to be the event of the century for this ranch, and it seemed as if everyone wanted to be here. Mr. O'Brien—being a rancher of renown, a gentleman, and a fantastic host—only led to more attendance than one could imagine. We had to build additional sleeping quarters for our guests. We went to Fossil and gathered up all the excess tents and paraphernalia that would be necessary for our dignitaries, and the local people that were coming, who had invited themselves to our gala, had to provide their own quarters. It was just not possible for the ranch to provide quarters for everyone. Mr. O'Brien and Bobby saw that the work on the ranch was still accomplished, even though the entire hullabaloo made it difficult. Not one cowboy complained about the extra work that it caused or the long hours it took to accomplish.

Most of the cowboys from the Double O Bar and many of the surrounding ranchers thought that this would be a perfect time for them to audition for the Buffalo Bill Show that was so popular. None of our crew had ever seen Cody's show but had read about it (those who could read) and saw that it was drawing large crowds in the thousands in the Eastern United States. Everyone wanted to see cowboys and Indians at their best—especially famous ones. Buffalo Bill Cody secured his nickname (Buffalo) when he worked for the railroad to bring in meat for the railroad crews that was building the continental railroad across the nation. He was reported to have brought 4,500+ fresh buffalo for the railroad crews in eighteen months—hence his name Buffalo Bill Cody. He was also a scout for the United States Army and an Indian fighter, pony express rider. He was awarded the Congressional Medal of Honor by Congress of the United States.

Mr. O'Brien sent Jack Sundown to Arlington, Oregon, where the railroad stopped. It was his duty to guide his friend Sitting Bull and the braves to the ranch, which might take three or four days as the only way to get to the Double O Bar ranch was by wagon or horseback. Sitting Bull had brought his braves and their horses in a railroad boxcars, unloaded them in Arlington with Jack's help, and headed for the Double O Bar ranch. It was a festive meeting between the two friends, not like when they had returned from Canada in defeat, to live on the Standing Rock Indian reservation. We were informed later that Sitting Bull told Jack that the only reason he had accepted Buffalo Bills show offer was that he had respect for Buffalo Bill, who was an honest man. The Indians had great respect for honesty. Indians were on their way to the ranch by the way of Fossil, Oregon; it created quite a stir in the town.

Buffalo Bill Cody's entourage arrived in Arlington, Oregon, a few days later. Leading the group was Buffalo Bill Cody and his white horse, Ishan. Buffalo Bill Cody was born February 26, 1846, died in 1917 of kidney failure. At fourteen he was appointed pony express rider. At the age of eighteen, he enlisted in the union Army, a man of high distinction. He was a scout for the US Army during the Indian wars, and the Indians had high respect for him. They knew him to be an honorable man. Buffalo Bill Cody also traveled down the main street of Fossil and drew an enormous crowd of the local residents. For the last four days, the people in the country had been arriving at the Double O Bar Ranch. They just didn't trickle in, but they came in by the dozens. They were coming by horseback by wagon by Prairie schooners and every means of travel that was possible. An event like this, as we said before, was a once in a lifetime. The headquarters of the ranch looks like a small city, and I'm sure it would grow even more.

Mr. O'Brien and his family were gracious hosts and was doing all they could to make the peoples stay enjoyable. Mr. O'Brien had sent Will to Arlington to meet Buffalo Bill and bring them all to the ranch—Will thrilled with the aspect of meeting in person Buffalo Bill Cody. Mr. O'Brien, for some reason which he did not say kept me close to the ranch. Maybe I was too young. I don't know. But I was happy to see and talk to Patricia more than normal because of the activity around the headquarters. Extra cooks had been hired, and the hands on the ranch that didn't have particular jobs at the time was told to help handle the crowd because who knew what people would do. A band had been hired for the event, and this was turning out to be one of the kind revelations.

The Indians came with Jack Sundown. They set up their teepees that they had brought about a quarter mile from headquarters. When all the settling was finished, Jack Sundance went to the headquarters and told Mr. O'Brien, myself, and others that the great visionary War Chief Sitting Bull would present himself to the O'Brien's in a few hours. He was in his tepee with his two squaws, who were traveling with him as usual, and was putting on his finest regalia. He felt that the owner of this great ranch was very courteous to allow him and his braves to stay on the ranch for a few days to renew his relationship with a true friend, Jack Sundown. We all waited in anticipation for the great chief.

When Sitting Bull did appear, he was followed by his squaws and his braves in a beautiful colorful column that no one could have expected. His war bonnet was made of many colored feathers. The close feathers to his head were eagle feathers, which were highly valued. It fitted snugly on his head and ran down his back touching the ground. This was the Indian way to honor a great chief. The braves were wearing their finest beaded buckskins with many colors, and his two wives were decked out in their finest. All this was to show their respect for Thomas O'Brien and his family. The people who had gathered there on the ranch were completely off guard an silent as the great visionary war chief and his people walked to the front porch of the home of the O'Brien's. No one spoke. They had a reverent respect for Chief Sitting Bull.

Sitting Bull raised his hand in the sign of peace. He started speaking in the Lakota Sioux language, and he was being translated by Jack Sundown.

"My friends," he began sweeping his right arm around, encompassing all in attendance, "I am called Sitting Bull, War Chief of the Lakota Sioux, but it was not always so. I was given this name chief, when I was fourteen years old, after a battle with the crow Indian nation. My father, Jumping Bull and my mother, Holy Door, named me at birth Jumping Badger. My name was changed to Sitting Bull after my coming-of-age vision. My ancestors and I and many who came before grew up in the Sacred Black Hills of Dakota, where our happy tribes lived in peace for thousands of years. We lived by our own tribal laws and the law of the Great Spirit, which is true and just. We did not want war. We gave up some of our sacred land to the white eyes, signed treaties that were continuously broken by the white eyes. We still did not go to war.

"Then the great white father in Washington said he wanted all of our land, for themselves and the yellow iron found on it, sending Yellow Hair Custer and his prospectors to our land to find the yellow iron, breaking the last treaty called the Laramie Treaty. They told us, upon threat of war, to give up our sacred land and go live on the white man's reservation. They said we must send our children to white man's school, learn the white man's ways, forget the ways of our fathers and grandfathers, plow the mother earth. They wanted our weapons turned over to the blue coats. These things we could not do. As any man worth his small ration of salt would do, even as the white eyes have done in their civil war, we fought for our freedom. My vision told of the defeat of the blue coats, all will die, but the white man did not believe my vision. We won the battle at greasy grass or Little Bighorn or Rosebud, whatever white man wants to call it, but later we lost our ancestral homes. Soldiers and hunters killed all of our buffalo. My people were starving. The soldier general said, 'The only good Indian is a dead Indian.' We can never return to our way of life, we must now bend as the willow tree in the storm, to the white man's way. I am going to Buffalo Bills Wild West show, I want the country to know the true story—that we were forced to fight the white man. I have no pleasure in the death of Yellow Hair Custer, and he never gave the Indians any quarter, so we gave him none. Thank you for your hospitality, Mr. O'Brien."

Sitting Bull turned and walked back to his village in silence, heads were bowed, and no one spoke.

I talked to Patricia later. She said that Sitting Bull's speech was heartfelt to her, and she felt very sorry for their people. I was happy to hear her say that because I too felt that way. To have to give up your home in that fashion would be heartbreaking. I asked Patricia why Mr. O'Brien kept me close to the ranch.

She said, "He knew you would protect me from harm, that you are fully capable of doing so." That made me feel a lot better than I had been.

Sitting Bull stayed at his village most of the time, and Jack Sundance was a frequent visitor to his tepee. They together, occasionally, walked up to the main house to visit with Tom O'Brien and family. Sitting Bull has said that Jack Sundown was a very good friend, so I guess all of our hands on the ranch had eaten their supply of crow.

William Fredrick Cody, in all his showmanship grandeur, came riding up the lane to the Double O Bar Ranch like the Pied Piper of Hamelin. He was followed by his entourage, and it seemed like half the people of Fossil. He was decked out in his finest attire, riding the beautiful, well-trained white horse, Ishan. Beside him rode Will on his beautiful Appaloosa stallion. They were a sight to behold, Buffalo Bill Cody's wife, Louisa Maud Frederici, was not with him on this trip. (They were married for fifty-six years until Cody's death in 1917.)

Cody rode his horse up to the O'Briens' front porch. The O'Briens had all come out of the house because they had heard his arrival. He was sitting there regally, and he doffed his plumed cowboy hat, and his horse knelt in a bow and everyone in the vicinity started clapping. You would have thought that it was the beginning of one of his Wild West Shows at the courtesy he was showing the O'Brien family. It was great.

He said, "Mr. O'Brien and your lovely family, I thank you for your generous hospitality for letting my people and I come here to meet with the great visionary War Chief Sitting Bull. He is a great man. With your permission, we would like to settle down for the night and prepare for a miniature show for Sitting Bull and his people and also for the people that have gathered here on this ranch to see Sitting Bull, and myself, if that meets your approval."

Mr. O'Brien said, "Yes, Mr. Cody, we have your quarters ready for your arrival."

We had a delightful supper. The invitees were Cody, Chief Sitting Bull, Jack Sundown, Bobby Chestnut, Will, and me. I enjoyed the heck out of it. Maybe my head was turned with all the dignitaries; besides, I got to sit beside Patricia. During supper, we talked about many items, and Cody spoke to Sitting Bull about the part that he and his braves would be playing in his show. It was an important part for Sitting Bull's to express his feelings about the subject and told Mr. Cody that occasionally and especially in front of heads of state. He would like to explain the Indians part of The Little Bighorn and the killing of Custer. As he said before, he took no pride that Custer was killed; he only did what was necessary at the time. All of us at the table were enthralled with our two guests.

The night passed in a wink of an eye. All the cowboys on the ranch and most of our guests were up and about waiting for the daily festivities. Mr. Cody wanted all the other cowboys that were going to perform to do that before any of his performers. All the guests that came on the ranch, we had them check their guns; so with the drinking of the cold beer, it was cold. Some of the cowboys had gone up into the mountains and brought back ice and had cooled the beer barrels, which was a treat for most of our guests.

We decided to have the shooting match first. The weapons were returned to the men who were going to enter the contest. The targets had been placed the night before, and it didn't take long to get everything in order. The long guns were first, and they were about fifteen participants. The handguns were next, and this was where I participated. It was a draw-and-fire contest—the same setup as before and the outcome was the same.

The rodeo had its riders, bareback horses, bull riders, bucking horses, bull dogging, calf roping, and various other contests. Again, Bobby Chestnut took the trophy. During the festivities, Patricia stood up and told me she needed to go to the house but she would only be gone a short time. I watched her go into the house. After about ten to fifteen minutes, she did not return, and I got uneasy. Major and I went through the house. I called, and she didn't answer, which made me even more uneasy. I told Major to fetch and put him on Patricia's scent, and he headed for the barn behind the house. I had turned my weapons back to the checker after my contest was over, so I had no pistol. I thought it was strange that Patricia would go to the barn. I was determined to find her. Major was going alone at a fast pace but not running. As we got closer to the barn, Major picked up the pace, and I was almost in a run to keep up. In going through the corridor between the stalls, I heard a faint cry, and I ran even faster. I got to the last stall, and I could hear what seemed like a ruckus, or fight, going on.

When I opened the stall door, I saw Patricia in the clutches between these two cowboys. She was fighting and clawing at their eyes, trying to get away. The cowboys were laughing and feeling her breasts, which made me furious. I reached for my knives, and in one motion, I threw both with all my strength at each of these persons. I didn't want to call them cowboys; they don't deserve the name. I hit each bastard in the desired area of their body. There could be no survival for them. I carried Patricia over to the arena; everyone rushed over to find out what was happening.

I told them what I knew—about missing her, searching the house, Major picking up her trail, searching the barn, hearing her cry, and seeing the bastards manhandling her. I killed them both with my knives. My dad would have been proud of me. Both bastards worked on the same ranch.

I thought, *Is this typical type of ranch hands that this rancher hires, and if so, are the rest of the crew the same? I want to do a little more investigation about this ranch and the crew. Did any of the rustlers work for this ranch?*

Jack Sundown, Will, Bobby, and other cowboys went to the barn to the back stall and dragged the two cowboys I had killed out by the heels into the middle of the arena. They were stone-dead cold each with a knife sticking out of his neck after it had severed the artery. It could be no doubt that my knives were the cause of their demise. I pulled my knives out of the two carcasses and cleaned them up and restored them to their sheaths. The cowboys in the bunkhouse could not believe the accuracy that I threw my knives, and they had no idea that I could use a knife so well and be so proficient—no one knew except Will—not Jack, not Bobby, not Mr. O'Brien, not Patricia, or no one. Will was my friend. This was getting alarming to me. Since Will and I met, he and I had thirteen—fourteen killings—and I didn't like that at all. I was catching up to Billy the Kid.

Mr. O'Brien, after we had gotten Patricia calmed down, said, "Bill, this is the second time that you have saved Patricia's life. It will not be forgotten by me or mine."

He asked Mr. Cody if the rodeo could be postponed until at least tomorrow so people on the ranch could come to grips with what's happened.

Buffalo Bill said, "Of course, by all means, no one could continue performance with this horrendous act hanging darkly over our heads."

I asked Bobby how long this rancher had been in this vicinity.

He said, "Couple of years."

Not that I believed in intuition, but some things were hard to explain, like Sitting Bull's vision. The rustling had started about two years ago, and the rustlers needed a venue to sell the stolen stock. If these two cowboys were any indication of the other riders on the ranch, this could be the reason and hopefully the solution. I told the three of them what I had been noodling around in my head.

"Perhaps a way to solve this rustling is staking out some of the surrounding land a week or so. Bobby, you must stay here and run the Double O Bar Ranch, but you will be in command. We will keep you in the loop when we know something. We'll take turns two nights each with supplies like airtights and jerky, we can't build fires, it may be seen, which could be devastating for one of us. Let's not tell Mr. O'Brien or his family of our intentions, we'll start as soon as this hullabaloo is over."

They all nodded their heads and said yes. I knew that this was a desperate move, but we had to follow any leads that showed its hideous face.

Next day I was asked by Buffalo Bill to show him my skills with a knife. He already knew my skills with a pistol and a rifle. I was a little embarrassed. Buffalo Bill had the targets set up himself; they were moving targets. Patricia had recovered enough from her ordeal to come with her mother and father to watch my demonstration, and I was hoping with all my heart that I would do a good job. I had no idea ever auditioning for Buffalo Bill's show. He was making it as difficult for me as possible because he knew if I could do this, I could do most anything, so I had to throw my knives off of my Appaloosa mare at a slow gallop. The cowboys from the bunkhouse were there, as well as Bobby, Jack, and Will. Will had never seen me throw the knives off of a galloping horse. He was a little apprehensive as well as I, but I thought to myself the show must go on, steel myself in my mind that I could do this; so with that determination, I healed my mare softly and began my run. It seemed so natural and so easy and so much fun, and I accomplished it easily. Everyone that was in the audience, including some people from the other ranches and from Fossil, were clapping and whistling. They had never seen a demonstration of knife-throwing like that. Buffalo Bill said it was the finest exhibition of knife throwing he had ever seen. I rode my Appaloosa up to the arena rail in front of Patricia and tipped my hat, showing that I did this for her, and she was smiling broadly.

I believe, that day, my reputation—good or bad—was made.

The next day, the Buffalo Bill show, limited, was put on at the Double O Bar arena. He had a few riders with him. They rode some of our ranch horses and a few of the ranch prize bulls, but really no one was better than our cowboys and especially Bobby. He still took all the trophies. Mr. Cody offered me $100 a month if I would go and star in a portion of his show throwing my knives. Hundred dollars is a lot of money, three times what a cowboy makes, so it was a tempting offer. He also offered Jack Sundown a position in his show, especially since Sitting Bull would like him to come. We both turned him down, and he said if we ever decide to leave the ranch, to come to his headquarters you have a job.

The word about the job offer was leaked to the O'Briens, and Patricia came to me and said, "I'm so happy that you did not accept Cody's offer, although it was a good one. The ranch would be a lonesome place without you."

I said, "Mr. O'Brien, I'm sorry I didn't ask you about my status as a cowboy here at your ranch. I guess I took things for granted, and I'm sorry I did so."

Mr. O'Brien said, "Bill, you'll always have a job here as long as you want it, and as long as I own this ranch, that won't change. I can't believe the skills that you have with the rifle, pistol-shooting, and the knife-throwing, for someone your age, and I'm sure that my wife and Patricia feel safer with you on the ranch."

"I'll always do my best, Mr. O'Brien," I said. "Thank you for your words of confidence!"

All our guests and dignitaries had left, leaving the ranch back to normal. All the cowboys enjoyed seeing and hearing the words of visionary War Chief Sitting Bull and the flamboyant style and words of Buffalo Bill Cody, but it was nice getting back to our ranch work. I suggested to Bobby that we start our plan on this new ranch owner and start surveillance on Friday night.

"Why on Friday night?" he asked.

"I don't know, except it would seem better for the ranch hands to be gone off the ranch for the weekend, like to town, than through the week, easier to hide their hidden agenda."

We flipped a coin to see which of the three of us would take the first watch. I guess I won, so I was packing up my gear and food, and I knew it was going to be a cold, dark, miserable two nights without hot food and especially Arbuckle coffee. Before dark, each day, if I could, I would boil some coffee so that the fire could not be seen and drink it cold if the opportunity presented itself. I found what I thought was a secure place to set up camp. I could see the ranch house and the out buildings quite well, so chances were that no one would be riding by, but my field of view was uninhibited.

I was in a corpse of small trees. It was dark inside with the shadows and leaves, but I could see out very well. Without being seen and with this unique pattern of the Appaloosa, she was almost indistinguishable. After two nights with no action, I was glad that my stakeout was over. As I slipped back into the OO Bar Ranch, I told Bobby what I had seen and not seen, where my stakeout was in the corpse of trees, and for him to assign Jack to the next available surveillance duty.

Next morning, I was out saddling up my Appaloosa when Patricia walked up and said, "Bill, would you take me for a ride?"

I said, "I'd love to, Patricia, but first I must get permission from Bobby. He's the ranch foreman, and he may have a chore for me to do this morning. I'll be right back."

Having gotten Bobby's permission, I saddled Patricia's horse.

She said, "I had the cook make up a picnic basket for us, we can ride longer than normal and not have to be back for dinner."

I said, "Patricia, I'm so happy you chose me to ride with you."

She said, "Bill, there is no other one on this ranch that I will ask but you."

I was happy to hear that but a little taken aback, not that I would ever take her affections for granted. In my wanderings on the ranch, I had run across a beautiful lake when I was riding out on the range. Would this lake be appropriate for our picnic? She said it would be as we rode along, side by side, over the upper reaches of the ranch. I was in heaven. We got to the limits we wanted. It was a sunny day, perfect for a picnic, so we chose a spot close to the water, ground-hitched our horses, and spread the cloth in the picnic basket that the cook had furnished.

The cook had fried some chicken and had made some potato salad and some dessert. The cook also must've had a little romance in her heart because she had slipped inside the picnic basket a small bottle of wine and two glasses. We talked about the ranch and other small talk. She asked me about my growing-up years, and I told her honestly what had gone on before I came to the ranch. I hadn't told her about the hobo camp, the boxcars, the hobos, including Will, about dodging the railroad bulls, when I was bored I would learn to use the knife as entertainment on the farm. I told her about Major, that the hobos wanted to add him to the Mulligan stew, so Major went out and he and I caught two rabbits for the Mulligan stew. I told her about Jim Galloway, the job that Will and I had on the irrigation ditch, and about Ray and his rattlesnake ordeal. I told her about Major finding the outlaws. They were going to hold up the Old Minnesota railroad. I told her about the fight and the capture of the outlaws. I told her about the shooting practice each day on the canal bank with Jim Galloway's furnishing free ammunition. I told her about the reward—the lifetime ticket on the railroad, the saving of the $58,000 payroll, the adventure of the Nez Perce Indian reservation and buying our Appaloosa horses, about the three outlaws who came into our camp; they were going to kill us for our horses and our goods. I told her about my desire to find Bobby, my first cousin, and live on a ranch.

I said, "Patricia, I think an awful lot of you, and I want you to know my history. Not too far in the future, I'm going to ask you an important question. I wanted you to know what I am before you make any hasty decisions. Let's become more than just friends. When each of us feel the time is right, we'll know what to do."

Patricia said, "Bill, I know what to do now. I don't have to wait, but I understand your position, and, yes, let's be more than just friends."

I reached over and drew her into my arms and kissed her soundly, pressing her body close to mine, saying, "This seals our bargain."

I said, "Patricia, I don't think we should tell your mom and dad our true feelings just yet, we're both young, and they may think this is a passing fad, but to me, it's the most important thing in my life. We'll explain to them when we decide what our destiny will be."

Riding back to the ranch, I felt so very close to Patricia. It was like knowing her and loving her all my life. I hoped she felt the same way. When I got back to the ranch, Bobby, Will, and Jack were waiting. I unsaddled Patricia's horse, gave him a rubdown, and turned him loose in the corral. Patricia looked at me in a knowing way and walked up to her house.

I turned to the boys and said, "What's up?"

Bobby said that Jack had hit pay dirt, four ranch hands had left the ranch and were traveling West. Jack said he followed them for half a day until he heard cattle bawling. He ground-tied his horse and sneaked up on them. They were feeding and watering the cattle in what looked like—he couldn't get a close enough look—a rebrand cattle pen. They were no other answer or reason for this to be happening.

Bobby said, "Okay, let's go talk to Mr. O'Brien and tell him of our suspicions."

Bobby went to the front door and knocked, and Patricia's mother came to the door. Bobby asked if Mr. O'Brien was available and said that we needed to speak to him. Mr. O'Brien was flabbergasted when we told him what we had done and what Jack had found. He asked Will to ride to another ranch. We wanted to have some other rancher as a witness to confront the rustlers. The rustlers have the same MO as the previous rustlers that we had caught and got killed before they could testify in court who the boss was. It seemed clear to us now that the additional information that had been brought by Jack was that the boss man must be the ranch owner and his henchmen must be the ones that killed the sheriff pro tem and the prisoners back in fossil.

Bobby explained to Mr. O'Brien that the stakeout was my idea and that I was suspicious of the rancher who had only been here a short time and then the rustlings began. Mr. O'Brien praised me for my intuition. The other rancher and four of his cowboys finally showed up on the ranch. Everything that we could explain, we did. We put the rancher and his hands up for the night so we could have an early start in the morning, Mr. O'Brien requested that I, Will, Jack, and Bobby go along with him and the other ranch owner and his cowboys. There might be gunplay, I thought; and most of all, I wanted to protect Mr. O'Brien and our crew when we apprehended the rustlers

There probably would be shooting as the rustlers know their potential outcome—hanging by the neck until they were dead, dead, dead. I suggested to Bobby and Mr. O'Brien that if the rustlers were not in camp, we should secure our positions and wait for their return. As it turned out, all four were in camp. There were ten of us against four. We were hoping that our overpowering numbers would keep them from putting up a fight, but it wasn't so. When the ruckus started, lead was flying in every direction. I tried to keep my horse between the rustlers and Mr. O'Brien. Will was the first one hit, and he flew out of the saddle. I shot and killed two of the cowboys. The other rancher shot one in the shoulder, painful but not serious; fourth was wounded by Mr. O'Brien. The ranchers cowboys took the wounded rustlers and tended, not too gently, to their wounds and tied them up. The ranchers and Bobby went to the corral along the creek and checked out the stolen cattle. Some were from the Double O Bar herd, some from the herd of the rancher that was with us, and others from the surrounding ranches. They had used their running iron on the cattle. Some were almost healed, and some were still raw from the burning, changing of the brands. We found the running iron lying in the burned-out branding fire, which we would use as definite proof, as well as the cattle that was rebranded an in the corral of the Double O Bar, which was the closest ranch to the rustlers' hideout. We secured the wounded outlaws in the same storage shed that we had kept the original outlaw, Henry, and put a guard on them.

As soon as the firefight was over, I attended to Will's wound. He had gotten hit in the left shoulder, but it was a flesh wound and had not broken any bones. It would heal quickly, but it was painful. He could dog it around the ranch for a few weeks, milk it as long as he could. Given notice, the other ranchers in the area gathered at the Double O Bar ranch. We decided that the best form of action was to take the three prisoners into Fossil and turn them over to the new sheriff. With the new sheriff in tow, we went out to the rancher's ranch and arrested him and his men for rustling and locked them up for trial. After being burnt once, we wanted to be very careful that our prisoners would not be shot again on a dark night. So the town council hired extra deputies to be on guard inside and outside the jail at all times, no more chances of the rustlers being shot. The circuit judge would be here in one week for this trial. Each cowboy was taken to a quiet room where he was interrogated to find out the details of this rustling ring. It was very revealing.

It seemed according to two of his men—I don't want to call them *cowboys*—that the ranch owner and they were just a hop and a jump away from being captured in another state. They had come out here to Oregon hoping to duplicate the rustling ring that they had in Idaho. We sent a telegram to Idaho, asking law enforcement to give us any details they could on the ranch owner and his men, anything that we could use for evidence in the trial that is coming up shortly.

Patricia and I met for a conference. I wanted to tell her in as much detail as possible what had happened when we encountered the rustlers. I told her that I wasn't avoiding her in any shape, form or fashion. It's just that things are happening so fast and we're trying to tie up all the loose ends against the rogue rancher and his henchmen. I told her that I tried to keep my horse and me between Mr. O'Brien and the rustlers so he would have less chance of being hit by any of the flying bullets during the fight. I told her that it was necessary for me to kill the two rustlers, but it wasn't something that I was proud of. I had not been proud of any killing that I'd had to do in my young life, and I wanted her to know how I felt.

She said that she understood perfectly my position and that she was a woman of the range and understood the duties that we cowboys had to perform even though it might be a distasteful event.

She said, "Bill, I was so worried about you. I know that you would be in the line of fire, you're that kind of person. I had my trepidations but faith in you as well. I knew you would come out on top, if just for me."

The traveling circuit judge came to town and began to set a trial date for the rustlers and the murderers. We had gathered an overwhelming pile of evidence against the rancher and his henchmen. They could be no mistake as to their guilt. The trial continued for two days. They had their own court-appointed attorney, so they had the full advantage of our wonderful Constitution. The jury was out only thirty minutes and returned with a guilty verdict on all counts. The judge went over all the evidence to try and find some redeeming cause but could find none. His sentence for murder and rustling was death by hanging, and it was to be performed the morning of the second day after sentencing. A scaffold had been made earlier that week that would accommodate four hanging nooses.

It was a sinister-looking scaffold. The town was overflowing with ranchers and cowboys from far and wide. Watching the hanging of these four men, we hoped would be a detriment for anyone else that had the same idea. We hoped we could keep the women away from the hanging, but we were unsuccessful. They had a mind of their own. A hanging was not a very pretty sight. They are marched up the thirteen steps to the gallows. The gallows were designed for thirteen steps—each step, eight inches high, that would give a total of eight-foot-six drop. When the trapdoor was thrown, it would leave enough distance to humanely break someone's neck and leave them hanging off the ground so they could be handled sufficiently to be taken to the burial destination.

The mornings of the hanging, the four men were led to the bottom of the stairway for the last thirteen steps of their lives. Some could hardly make the stairs, stumbling and weeping and hollering—some for their mothers—"I don't want to die." But they listened to the criminal music, and now they must pay the fiddler. When they died, they defecated involuntarily on themselves, which was an odorous and unsightly mess.

Everyone hoped that this hanging would be the last and there would be no more rustling in the area. But each of us knew down in our hearts that greed would someday raise its ugly head again and all this would be of no consequence. But in the meantime, life and ranching must go on.

It seemed that the hands on the ranch had a different kind of respect for Will, Jack, and me. It was only my own feelings. Two days later, the four of us—Bobby, Jack, Will, and I was again invited to the main house for supper. I believed the O'Briens wanted to have a talk with us.

As we were sitting around the table and after Mrs. O'Brien said grace, and before the food was served by the cook—she brought us coffee and we were sipping on that—Mr. O'Brien said, "Boys, I want to make a point to thank the four of you for what you did for this ranch, which was far beyond the call of duty. No ranch owner could or would expect their cowboys to put themselves in harm's way. What the four of you have accomplished here in this Eastern Oregon vicinity is awesome. To have the four of you working on this one ranch, I consider it a privilege. My whole family feels the way I do. And, Bill, you especially, having put yourself in harm's way, putting yourself between me and the rustlers so I wouldn't get injured is deeply felt. You four have my sincere gratitude and my unwavering respect."

Each of us cowboys sitting at the table were overcome by the praise, each of us acknowledging to ourselves it was an embarrassing moment but deeply appreciated. Patricia was looking at me, and her eyes were beaming. Her mother probably saw that look also. I was feeling a little uneasy, and my shirt collar seemed to be a little tighter listening to all the praise.

After supper, when we were leaving the main house walking toward the bunkhouse, Bobby took me aside and said, "Bill, I had no idea when we were young, back on the farm, that you would turn out as you have. You were taught by your father what's right and what's wrong and a work ethic that will stand you well the rest of your life. I just want you to know, like Mr. O'Brien, that I'm proud of you."

I said, "Bobby coming from you, that's high praise."

The town Council of Fossil approved a banner across the main street, saying in large letters, "Beware, rustlers are hanged in this town." It was a true and plain statement. In all of my fandangos that I'd been doing lately, Major was right by my side. He was a faithful partner to have along with you. Patricia and the cook see to it that Major had plenty to eat and he was well cared for. None of us ever diminished the feats that he had accomplished; he is one of the ranch's "cowboys"!

The weather was getting warmer, and the cattle were putting on weight, eating the new nutritious grass and soon will be time to drive the herd to Arlington, Oregon, which was the railhead for shipping the cattle east. We were supplying a great herd of the beast to the Chicago feed lots and slaughterhouses. This was not like the cattle drives of old, when it took months to drive the cattle to the nearest railhead, but it did have its ups and downs at times. I was still looking forward to the cattle drive.

I had never been on one before. All I had been doing was fantasizing—when I was reading the dime novels that Edward Zane Carroll Judson Junior, *Alias*, Ned Buntline was writing about in the early West. In those penny deadfalls, Buntline had Indians, rustlers, storms, flooded rivers, brushfires, disease, stampedes, other catastrophes that a young man could fantasize about and dream his dreams, place himself in that category, make himself a hero, while he was snug in his blanket. We would be driving in the neighborhood of 7,800 steers to the market this time—quite a chore getting that many cattle safely to the railhead. Bobby thought that we had enough cowboys to handle the drive, but Mr. O'Brien decided to hire eight more Mexican vaqueros to help us out. Vaqueros are excellent horsemen, and they knew cattle well. They were good workers, and if you treated them honestly, they would be friends of yours forever.

One of the vaqueros played the Spanish guitar beautifully and had an excellent voice. Some of my favorite music was played on the Spanish guitar. This Vaquero was an artist and, I believed, should be performing his music for the entertainment of others and get well compensated. But it was hard for a Mexican to catch a break and get ahead from the ranch life; he was also a dedicated vaquero. From the ranch to the railroad and Arlington, it was, as the crow flew, about hundred and ten to fifteen miles; and driving the cattle, we should make between fifteen to twenty miles a day, so total of six or seven days to reach our railhead. That was not a very long cattle drive, so the women wanted to go on the drive with us, branch off, and go on to Portland for a shopping spree. The women needed to get out occasionally and stretch their legs and buy their necessities, and Portland was a large enough town to get almost everything they need. Bobby left a skeleton crew on the ranch to see that everything was accomplished while we were gone. We didn't try to trail brand the herd; it was such a short drive.

Since Will and I were the newest cowboys, we chose—with Bobby's insistence—to ride drag with four of the new vaqueros. One of the vaqueros that were riding drag with us was the one that played and sang the beautiful Mexican ballads. He and I got friendly on the trail the first day. I told him of my appreciation of the Spanish guitar and Mexican ballads. I said I would appreciate it, if tonight after supper he would play for the senora and senorita some of his beautiful music. He said he would be delighted to play for someone of their beauty. The vaqueros were always romantic. I told him in secrecy that Patricia and I had unintentionally fallen in love and play that ballad that I had heard him play before.

He immediately said, "Yes, I have a new song that I would like to play and sing for them."

"Bueno," I said.

After supper that night, the cattle had quieted down, I walked over to Mr. O'Brien and said, "Mr. O'Brien I have a treat for you and your wife and Patricia if you would please come over and sit with me. I have a vaquero that's a real artist with a Spanish guitar and has a beautiful voice, I have asked him to serenade you and your family with a few songs."

Mr. O'Brien said, "That's wonderful, Bill. I'm sure the ladies and I will enjoy it immensely."

I walked over to the vaquero and said, "We're ready if you are."

He said, "It is my pleasure, senor."

He walked over to where the O'Brien family was sitting, and out of his guitar rose a haunting beautiful medley, which he played with grace and accomplishment. The noise around the camp suddenly became extremely quiet as the beautiful notes from the guitar lifted gently and tenderly into the air, covering the entire camp. It was uncommonly beautiful. He played other songs and sang them with his outstanding voice.

He then walked over to Patricia and said, "Senor Bill dedicates this song to you, senorita, this is a song I have just written for you, and I want you and your family to hear it for its premier."

As he sang and played the song, it had a life of its own, and you could tell that the writer and singer had felt this heart breaking injustice himself, that he was hurt deeply beyond repair, and he was looking for a way to suppress and control his broken heart. As the last notes reverberated, slowly faded into night, you could see the look on everyone's faces—especially the girls and the glistening in their eyes. The song was a huge success and should be played on the world's stage. The artist was praised—and make no mistake, he was an artist—and as we all went to bed, we kept hearing the wonderful music in our heads. I silently vowed to myself to help him make his music known.

Next morning at breakfast, Patricia and her mother came over to me and said, "Bill, last night was one of the most enjoyable nights we have spent in a long time. That vaquero should enjoy a life of music and exclaim, he is too important to the entire Mexican community to be allowed the chance of being hurt working cattle, although he does like his job."

Patricia said, "Bill, that was the most beautiful, heartfelt song I have ever heard. Thanks for giving us the opportunity to hear it."

"De nada," I said.

When we got to the railhead, Mr. O'Brien had reserved the corrals and drove his cattle through the gates and had two counter tallies—one from the buyer and one from the ranch. As a cow would go through the gate, the tally counter would tie a knot in the small lariat. Each knot represented twenty cattle. We had a total of 7,865 steers—which, at the negotiated price of $22 each, was a lot of money. He took the cashier's check from the slaughterhouse agent and deposited it in his bank in Arlington. The cattle drive was over for the year. The men were paid their salary, including the eight vaqueros, and they had free reign for two days and then headed back to the Double O Bar. I sent a telegram to Buffalo Bill Cody, telling him of the vaquero, that he could play the Spanish guitar so beautifully and sing and write songs as well, would he please have a place in his show for an act of this caliber, and that all on the Double O Bar felt that he would be extremely happy if he hired this vaquero.

Next afternoon, I received a telegram from Buffalo Bill, saying, "Send this vaquero immediately to my show, with your recommendation, and I know that it will be a successful partnership."

We were all happy, and especially José, he could not thank us enough for his good fortune.

The two days was over, and the ranch hands, including Mr. O'Brien, were heading out the next morning for the ranch.

He came to me and said, "Bill, the women are catching the train to Portland for a shopping spree, I would like for you to escort them on this trip. I trust you implicitly to take care of them, if the need arises."

I said, "Mr. O'Brien, I'll do the best I can, but I request that Will go along with me also. He is very loyal to you and your family, as well as a good friend of mine."

Mr. O'Brien said, "Certainly, I'll tell Bobby that you two are indisposed until the women are back on the ranch. Here's some walking-around money while you're gone," as he handed me an envelope.

Will and I had never been to the large city before. The population at this time was around two hundred thousand people. We had to keep on our toes and be sure the women were not harmed or molested.

On the train ride to Portland and when we reached our hotel destination, we booked rooms across the hall from Patricia and her mother. As this was an upper-class hotel, we had some difficulty getting the manager to allow Major to stay in our room, but we explained that he was a member of the family and he had to stay in our room. The manager finally accepted that with a little enumeration or monetary persuasion, whichever. I went down to the hotel clerk later that evening and asked him if there was public transportation that could be acquired. The ladies wanted to go to the shopping district and spend some time in the stores. He said that he could have a carriage available to the ladies and us at ten o'clock the next morning. That evening, after supper, I told them about my arrangement, and they said they would be ready at ten o'clock next morning. We stayed close to their hotel room for the rest of the evening.

Next morning, Will and I were up early, as we normally did on the ranch. At eight o'clock that morning, we decided we would go to their room to wake them up so they could have breakfast before the ten o'clock transportation arrived. We went to the room and knocked on the door but got no answer. We knocked again and waited five minutes and then became concerned. We saw a housemaid down the hall, and we asked her to open the door with her passkey to the ladies' room and see if they were okay. She did and came back out and said no one was there. We couldn't believe what we were hearing. Will and I stormed into the room, looked around, and saw no sign of the two women. There were no clothes or apparel of any kind. The room was empty. Where were the women that were in this room?

She answered, "There have been no women in this room. It has been vacant for the last two days."

We were dumbfounded and hurried down to the clerk at the desk. We asked him where the women were.

"No," he said, "what women? There have been no women in that room."

We asked for the register. He showed us the register. We saw our names where we had signed, but the women's names were not there. They had been removed somehow. We could see that we couldn't get any help from the clerk, so we went to the local police station and reported the missing women. We told the police exactly what had happened, and they went to the hotel with us. We checked with the restaurant staff, and they too said at supper last night that only the two men were there. A mass conspiracy was in place.

I immediately went to the telegraph office and wired the Double O Bar ranch:

> "Attention, Bobby Chestnut, women miss-
> ing, and no help from police. Bring Mr. O'Brien
> and Jack with you, and come immediately."

Mr. O'Brien knew the hotel where we were staying; he had made the reservations. We had heard nothing the evening before, nor did we hear anything last night or this morning. It had been completely silent. Major had heard nothing either, so he did not sound the alarm. Will and I sat in the lobby of the hotel, discussing the circumstances, trying to piece together what could've happened and where the women were. When ten o'clock rolled around, the transportation vehicle did not appear. That gave us our first clue as to who might be involved in the kidnapping.

A bellboy came over to our table with an envelope and said, "This was placed in your mailbox, and the desk clerk thought it may be important to deliver to you."

We opened the envelope and read the message. It said, "We have the two women. They are unhurt and will be delivered back to you after we receive $50,000 in small bills. Nothing larger than a $50 bill is to be given. We know of your cattle sale. We know you have the money in the bank, you have two days to deliver the cash at the assigned location, which we will tell you later. Do not go to the police."

"So here it is, a kidnapping, and there must be several people involved," I told Will. "We must interrogate all that we believe may be involved. We must use our own discretion as to how severely we question them, if you get my meaning."

He agreed.

I said, "Will, we need to talk to the clerk that signed us up yesterday and made the appointment today. Transportation for today did not show, so he and the driver must know that the women would not need their services. So to me, that meant that he has inside information and the clerk does as well, let's find his home address so we can interrogate him without being disturbed."

We asked the clerk if the late afternoon and evening clerk was married.

He said, "No, he's a single man."

And then Will asked him where he lived so we could deliver a letter to him in answer to the letter we had just received. We had to tell him something not to arouse any suspicion.

He gave us his address, and we hired a buggy to take us to his house. We knocked on his door, and when he opened the door, he was taken aback at seeing us at his door. We shoved him inside, closed the door, and said we needed to talk, earnestly.

I pulled my knife out of my belt sheath, and I said, in a tone of voice that he could not help but understand, "Where are the women?"

He denied knowing what we were talking about. He thought that he could explain away the fact that the women were missing. I walked over to him. We had him tied to a chair so he couldn't move a muscle, and I made a small slice on his earlobe, which started bleeding profusely. You would have thought I'd cut his throat by the sight of that much blood.

I said, "You can do much, much better than that to save your entire ear, and if that doesn't give you incentive to speak, I'll cut off your nose, and if you're still quiet, I'll cut off your other ear. And if that doesn't work, I'll cut off your upper lip. And if you're not going to use your tongue to talk, then I guess you don't need it, so the next thing I'll do is cut out your tongue. I want you to know I'm serious, and I'll go to any extreme on your body to make you talk, even your manhood. We are cowboys, and we know how to make bulls into steers, you get my meaning."

He started talking like a magpie. He knew I was serious. I wasn't playing around. He said that he was a member of a gang that kidnapped women to be sold on the slave market in Mexico and other countries. We asked how many times he had carried out this revolting act. He said maybe ten or twelve times.

"We were going to take your ransom money but not return the women to you but sell them for more money."

He pointed out that the ladies that had the right kind of looks and not traveling with a man in their rooms were targets. He notified the men who ran the transportation equipment for the hotel, and the gang came in and kidnapped the women out of the room. He said that the women were not harmed or molested before they were sold to the buyers because that damaged the goods and the price would be less. I told him that we wanted the names of everyone involved in this women-trafficking business, and we wanted it now.

"I want names, addresses, how long they've been doing this trafficking, and above all, I want to know where the two women are right now."

We got all the information that we wanted, and we had him sign a written confession. Will and I decided to move this piece of crap to another location just in case his band of cutthroats tried to find him, when he didn't show up for his counter duty at the hotel. We had seen some abandoned houses along the railroad as we were coming in to Portland, and we took him to one of those. We tied him securely and waited for the night to pass and the arrival of Mr. O'Brien, Bobby, and Jack. I sent Will out to locate some food and some drinks to bring back to our temporary hideout. I was taking no chances on this piece of crap getting away. Will had picked up a couple of blankets; I never did ask him where. When he bought the food, we ate, we drank what we thought was prudent, got under our blankets, and slept the night out. We were pretty sure that the women's safety was not being jeopardized at this point. We didn't know how many men were in the gang. We did know that a police officer was involved, and we could not put our information, our lives, and the women's lives, in jeopardy by notifying the police. It was to wait for our friends to arrive.

And arrive they did. You never saw three men so angry before. I had left Will in charge of the prisoner, and I had gone back to the hotel where all this charade had started. I told them every detail that I could remember. I showed them the desk clerks signed confession. I showed them the ransom note, and I told them what I had done to the desk clerk in getting the answers that I wanted. Jack Sundown and all there were furious and wanted to go see our prisoner immediately.

I rented another Surrey and took them to our hideout. Will was waiting with his gun in his hand. He had heard someone coming, and taking no chances, he had hidden and pulled his weapon, ready to defend the situation if necessary.

Mr. O'Brien went over to the prisoner and said, "You're lucky you're still alive, you don't deserve to be alive, and you may not be alive long in the future, but right now, we need additional information. I'm turning you over to my Indian friend, and he's going to ask you some pointed questions. My advice to you is answer truthfully and quickly."

Jack asked him all of the important questions needed to rescue the two women. We found out from our snitch that there were seven men in this band of cutthroats and the location where they were keeping the two women.

The two women was about five blocks from here. We didn't want to alarm the kidnappers, so we decided we would walk secretly to the hideout. We didn't want to hamper ourselves with our prisoner, so we decided to hide him among the rubble of this deserted house and leave him there for future questioning. I asked Jack if he could tie this piece of crap so he couldn't get away in a million years, and he laughed and said just, "Watch, Bill," and I did. Nothing could get loose the way Jack tied him up.

We then walked to where the gang was holding Patricia and her mother. I told Bobby, Jack, and Mr. O'Brien that Will and I should hang back a ways because they might have seen us at the hotel and recognized us, which would be detrimental to rescuing the women and not alarming the gang to soon.

We found the location, decided to put a plan in motion quickly. We sent Will and Bobby and Jack around to one side of the building, where a side door could be opened. Bobby took that and Jack and Will to the rear door. Mr. O'Brien and I were going in the front door.

I said, "Mr. O'Brien, I'm shooting to kill these dogs. They don't need to live in our world."

He said, "Bill, you're right. I'm with you."

We burst in the front door, shooting as we went. They scattered like rats going in every direction. Mr. O'Brien and I each killed one of the kidnappers, and I could hear shooting at the side door and also the rear door, and I knew Bobby, Will, and Jack were more than doing their job. Two kidnappers were wounded but alive. Mr. O'Brien and I rushed into the bedroom, and there lying on the bed tied were Mrs. O'Brien and Patricia.

Patricia looked at me and said, "Bill, I knew you'd come and save us."

I was over by the bed untying Patricia, and Mr. O'Brien was on the other side untying his wife. There was tears and gratitude filling the room with love.

Mr. O'Brien told our men to keep what was left of the gang secure until we got back. We took the women and their luggage to a different hotel and registered them. We told the desk clerk that we wanted no funny business, and we told him what had happened at the other hotel briefly.

Their clerk assured us that his hotel was strictly on the up and up, and I told him, "You had better be on the up and up, or you'll answer to me."

We made sure that the women were secure, and then Mr. O Brian and I went to the local police station. We asked to see the officer in charge of the station and told him we wish to talk in private. We introduced ourselves, and I, closest to the happenings, explained our situation. I told him about the crooked hotel, the crooked desk clerk, the crooked policeman, the crooked personnel carrier, the ransom note, the signed confession, location of the remaining crooks under guard by our men.

He said, "My god, the police force has been looking for these crooks for months but couldn't find anything. Here you cowboys come into town and was here only two days and solved our mystery and got back the hostages. You tell me that there have been ten or twelve kidnappings out of that hotel in the past few years, this is astounding news, and good work on your part. Let's go to your holding area and pick up these crooks."

I spoke up and said, "You had better bring your undertaker, as we did not take all of them alive."

He looked at me and Mr. O'Brien for several minutes and said, "Yes, I'll do that. I'll send word to the policeman's captain to pick him up and bring him here to this precinct so he can be questioned with all the living participants."

The undertaker brought his meat wagon, and the police captain brought his paddy wagon along with two other officers, and we went to the abandoned house where we were holding the prisoners. The captain and his two officers loaded them into the paddy wagon after handcuffing them and putting a leg chain on them. Also, a couple was wounded, and our cowboys had treated them as best they could; and when arriving at the police station, they would be treated by a real physician. After their wounds were taken care of came the grilling. One by one they were questioned about their operation and who was involved. The policeman was especially grilled, as he was a dirty cop.

We then, along with the police captain, went to the other hotel where the women were staying, and they too were questioned about the events. The women told of their ordeal with no modesty, telling it like it was. They had not been harmed physically other than a little feeling of their privates. They were told what their fate was going to be. It wasn't pretty. The two police captains doing the interrogation were satisfied with the women's statement, had them sign the statement, and said, "You're free to go."

No question the women were upset, but being women of the West, they recovered quickly and said that they wanted to continue their shopping since they were already in Portland and they might not get another chance for quite some time. All of us stayed in Portland for two more days before we caught the train back to Arlington.

A crime reporter who was at the police station when they brought in the crooks started asking questions about the arrests— why they were arrested and all questions that reporters ask. The captain knew the reporter well, and as the reporter asked the questions, the captain told him what he knew so far. He told the reporter that we cowboys had broken the sex slave ring that had been plaguing Portland for quite some time. He told him that there was a dirty cop involved and a dirty desk clerk who worked at the upper-class hotel was involved. He told about the kidnappers and their names and who he was holding in his jail and the names of the ones that the cowboys had killed. He did not tell them the name of the two women; he just said it was a mother and daughter kidnapped who was rescued and returned to their family. All the news that this reporter could gather was printed in the Portland paper and picked up by other newspapers in the rest of the United States. The ship captain and his crew were also arrested, and their contacts in Mexico were given to the Mexican government, which we could only hope the government would put in jail. The reporter learned the background of me and my friend Will. The reporter uncovered Bill and Will's exploits, before they came to the Double O Bar Ranch. It was a tantalizing story, which turned the cowboys into instant heroes. We spontaneously became heroes like a modern-day Sherlock Holmes and Watson. Everyone knows how reporters embellish a good tale of sex, crime, and murder. The reporter had also mentioned in his lengthy article that Bobby Chestnut, Jack Sundance, and Thomas O'Brien played an important part in this dastardly game and of bringing it to a well done conclusion. When we returned to Fossil, we were held as heroes by the mayor, city council, and a lot of the residents of the town. We had telegrams that had been sent to congratulate us by Buffalo Bill Cody, which said "Well done," telegram from Jim Galloway expressing his delight, president of the Old Great Northern Minnesota railroad (James J. Hill), which said "bully," or (great.)

The ladies had bought everything they needed, I suspect, because we had to hire two wagons out of Arlington to carry their purchases and us cowboys back to the Double O Bar Ranch. First chance we had to speak alone with each other, Patricia and I spoke of the ordeal that she and her mother had gone through in Portland. I told her that I was very sorry not to have found them sooner and stopped some of the rude actions that they were forced to endure.

She said, "Bill, no one could have done it faster or better than you and Will. I kept telling Mom not to worry, that I knew with a woman's premonition, that you would rescue us before it was too late. I believe that she knows now how we feel about each other, and I'm sure she's going to tell Dad."

I said, "Patricia, that may mean I have to leave the ranch for a time, they may think we're too young to know our own minds."

Patricia said, "No, Bill. I won't let that happen."

We were back at the ranch, trying to get into the rhythm of ranch life. It was a good life, and the camaraderie was great with all the hands. The summer was slipping up on us, as was the date for the Pendleton Roundup. The Roundup had grown from competition between a few ranches in the vicinity to a state wide rodeo in 1912 and gotten a lot larger. Still Bobby and Jack Sundown were going to compete for the Double O Bar Ranch. The prizes and money wasn't large; it was for the honor of the ranch.

The time had come. We were packing up, heading for the Pendleton Roundup. The cowboys that were contestants have their special gear packed. Exuberance prevailed throughout the ranks of the cowboys. This was the time they had been waiting for. Bobby and Jack were at the prime of their lives. Each was getting older, and they knew that not many years from now their physical abilities would slow down. So now they were up and ready to give their best. The ranch was in total euphoria. A skeleton crew was being left to operate the ranch; they drew straws to see who would stay at home. Money was passed, and some were bought off on who would stay and who would go; the price was high. This was not like the Buffalo Bill Cody Wild West show. This was real cowboys showing their stuff, their fifteen minutes of fame and glory. After a year of hardships and practice, this was their time to be somebody and maybe get to meet some girls at the rodeo, which was every cowboy's dream. They were going to do their level best.

Mr. O'Brien asked if he could have a discussion with me after returning to the Double O Bar Ranch.

I said, "Yes, sir, anytime." I said to myself, *Here it comes, as anticipated.*

He said, "Let's make it Saturday evening after we have our supper, to which you are invited."

I said, "I'll be there."

Mr. O'Brien had requested that Bobby, Jack, Will, and I be present. He said that he wanted each of my friends there and hoped that they would understand what was going to be discussed after supper. Patricia and I knew what was going to take place down deep in our hearts, and we were dreading the discussion.

After supper, when Mr. O'Brien started to talk, I said, "Excuse me, Mr. O'Brien, I would like to speak first." I said, "Patricia, is it all right with you if I speak for both of us?"

She said, "You know it is, Bill."

I said, "Mrs. O'Brien, Mr. O'Brien, let me tell you each our story that includes you Bobby, you Jack, and you Will, before any accusations of any kind are made—which we all may be sorry for later in life. First and foremost, without an inch of doubt, Patricia and I were in love. It was not an intentional thing. It just happened. This love of ours is not a carnal love, not for a moment. It's a lasting love, which will endure for an eternity. Neither of us has expressed any desire to take things any farther. We both know and have discussed our young age and your feelings as parents for your beautiful daughter. You want the best for her, and so do I.

"She is the first and only girl I've ever kissed, and that was only a kiss of lasting friendship and understanding. I would give my life for her, if the need arises, and she for me. We would not disgrace your parenting and your love for her. We have not done anything physical, and the love between us has always been honest, you two have taught her well. All of us sitting in this room know the physical drive and attraction and the desire and the fulfillment of sex, as God has made us beings, to continue to populate the earth, but Patricia and I know that we must abstain before marriage, and with difficulty, we have agreed to this together. Patricia, have I said anything that is not in your heart also?"

"No, Bill, you have expressed my feelings beautifully."

"Mrs. O'Brien, Mr. O'Brien," I said, "if you want me to leave, I bow to your wishes. I hope you will allow Patricia to write me when I have an address for her letters to reach me. I would like to stay until after Bobby and Jack's rodeo is over, as I have great feelings for both. And, Patricia, I will be back."

She said, "Oh, Bill," loudly and got up and left the room.

Mr. O' Brian said, "Of course, you can stay for now."

We cowboys stood up and tipped our hats and left the room.

Back at the bunkhouse, the four of us sat in Bobby's office and discussed what had happened at supper and the fact that even after my explanation of the relationship between Patricia and me, he still wanted me to leave the ranch.

It was like, "What have you done for me today?"

I just couldn't believe it. When I had first come to the ranch, I had no intention of staying. I only wanted to visit and renew my friendship with Bobby, and I got lucky, for me, I guess, Patricia was there to take my interest, but you would think after all that had happened—the rustlers, the ranch rodeo, the molesters, the saving of Patricia and her mother from the slave traders and so on—that it should have a bearing on Mr. O'Brien's outlook, but evidently it did not.

We talked into the night, trying to find a solution to this unusual—to say the least—situation. I told Bobby and Jack that I intended to stay until their rodeo performance was over, and in the meantime, I would put out some résumés and my attributes to the president of the old Minnesota railroad, to some of the sheriffs in the general and greater vicinity, to Buffalo Bill Cody, and others to see if they could use someone like me. I'll be at loose ends, footloose, and fancy-free after the rodeo was over. I wanted to keep in touch with all my friends that had gathered around me here so I could tell them my new adventures, such as they might be. Some of the other cowboys on the ranch said I was getting a raw deal and that they were going to quit the ranch, but Bobby and I told them that they had a good job and should stay working on the ranch instead of messing around with me. I knew not where I was headed. Will and Jack said that whatever I decided, they would go along with me. They wanted us to stay together on any job we chose to accomplish. I told them that as much as I welcomed their enthusiasm to go with me, it really wasn't necessary. If they thought the ranch was the best place for them, I could go it alone. They would not listen to that idea.

Bobby had given me my assignment for the day and told me to go check out the yearling calves on the south range to see if the water-hole was still holding water and that the fence was still in place and had not been knocked down. As I was going about my assignment, I saw Patricia on Blackie, heading in my direction. Bobby had settled Blackie down some and had shortened the horse's headstall to where he could not get the bit between his teeth. She would now be able to control Blackie a lot better. I turned my horse in her direction, and she stopped under a scrub oak tree, which still had some of its beau-tiful-colored autumn leaves hanging on the limbs.

As I rode up to the tree, I thought to myself, *What a beautiful sight.*

Patricia was on her black horse under this beautiful scrub oak tree. She and I jumped off our horses and left the reins on the ground. As we embraced, she was crying, and it was all that I could do to hold back my manly tears. We both sat on a nearby rock close together and told each other our thoughts and our wishes and our desires. We both knew that we were just making idle conversation, and at this point, none of those would come true. She was so upset with her father and mother—mostly her father—but I explained that I would feel the same way if she and I had a daughter in the same circumstances. I would be overprotective as well. I explained to Patricia that her father was a little overprotective of her and that we truly were young, but we knew and felt what was right between us, and it was for her parents' peace of mind. I told her of the talks that Bobby, Will, Jack, and I had and some of the expressions that the cowboys had of this idea of me leaving the ranch. I told her that this was destined to happen and that it would not make us lose our friendship and love for each other. I told her I had to leave after the rodeo and what I had done to try and find another job—hopefully in this locality, where I could ride for a few days and see her. But if that didn't happen, I would stay in touch as much as possible, and I requested that she write me whenever she thought of me.

This was the most serious talk I had with anyone except, in my young days, with my father about the rights and the wrongs that people did to each other, and most of them were done unintentionally. I told her I was staying until the rodeo was over and that we would see each other hopefully many times during that time, but we must still hold to our earlier values to abstain from any physical attraction until we were married, and that was going to be as soon as she and I became of consensual age. We sat on the rock with our arms entwined, knowing that this might be the last time for some months—or maybe a year, or maybe ever. It was a heartbreaking but glorious time, as long as we were with each other. We lost track of time. It passed so swiftly and started becoming late evening, and I told Patricia she must go home now and that I would certainly see her again. I thanked her, and I kissed her lovingly and gently on her full, delicious lips. I told her I would ride part of the way back to the ranch with her because I had done what Bobby had told me to do. Both knew that our togetherness was not over—could not be over; we would not let it be over—as we said our goodbyes.

Will and I had saved most of our money from the rewards and the bounties that we had collected before we arrived at the ranch. And we had spent very little of our money on that hellacious trip to Portland and most of our pay at the ranch had been put in the local bank, so financially, we were in good shape. We could lollygag around for six months or so without any concern of unemployment, so we told Bobby to take us off the payroll, but if he didn't mind, we would like to use the bunkhouse until after the rodeo was over. He said that that was understood between him and Mr. O'Brien and that we would stay at the bunkhouse and take our meals there on the ranch until we left.

Bobby said, "The day the three of you leave will be a sad day for the ranch and especially a bad day for me."

I told Bobby that I also regretted leaving, that he was the only living relative that I had left, and that I certainly wanted to keep in touch.

The day arrived when all the cowboys from the ranch except a skeleton crew left for Pendleton, Oregon. It was seventy miles to Fossil, Oregon, and 129 miles farther to Pendleton. The mode of travel was stagecoach, wagon, or horseback. Will, Jack, and I decided to ride our horses and stop off at Fossil, Oregon, for some R and R (which meant rest and relaxation). Before we traveled on to the rodeo, we had taken all of our gear with us because we had no idea what was going to happen after the rodeo was over. I had not heard back from any of my contacts about a job. We knew as we left the ranch gate, as each of us turned around in the saddle and looked at the ranch, that it would be a long time before we would be returning—if ever. No one knew what fate had in store. Our hearts were heavy. That night around our campfire, it was not as jovial and uplifting experience that camping out under the stars usually caused. I constantly kept telling Will and Jack that they did not have to babysit me. I was old enough and prepared enough to take care of myself. They would hear none of that kind of talk.

We got a room at the local hotel for two nights. Of course, this included Major. We decided to clean up, use the hotel facilities, have a good supper, and go to the saloon for some entertainment. We were minding our own business sitting quietly, having our drinks. Of course, I didn't drink liquor, so I was having iced coffee, when there was a disturbance across the room.

We looked at the room, and there were five cowboys sitting at a table, and you could see that they were drinking heavily. A couple of the cowboys were getting belligerent, even with their friends. It looked like trouble was brewing, and we didn't want to get involved in their arguments. We waved to the bartender to come over to our table and bring another round of drinks, solely so we could ask him who they were and what was transpiring. He said that they were a rowdy crew from another ranch that was going to be contestants at the Pendleton

Roundup Rodeo. They must have recognized Jack Sundance because Will and I had never been to the Pendleton Roundup before. Some people, when they get a snoot full of liquor, they lose all their rational thinking. I was not against having a drink, but one must drink responsibly and not let it take control of your senses.

They were getting louder and more boisterous as the evening progressed. We three decided that we had enough fun for one night. We had rode a long distance, and we would just retire for the night.

As we scraped back our chairs to get up from the table, one of the cowboys staggered over and accosted Jack, saying, "Are you the dog-eating Indian that's going to be a contestant at the roundup?"

Jack just stood there, looking at this cowboy, saying nothing—which, evidently, they mistook to be a sign of cowardice. When the cowboy stepped up into Jack's face and called him another derogatory name, Jack hit him with a full-body haymaker—knocking him stumbling, entangling in his own legs, and feet falling all over the floor back into his friends' table. His friends were just drunk enough that they decided they wanted a piece of the action, and so here came a donnybrook.

It was five drunken cowboys against three sober cowboys; it really wasn't much of a fight. We were holding our own—and perhaps better than holding our own—when one of the cowboys went for his gun. I threw my belt knife so quickly that no one saw my movement, and I hit him in the wrist, stopping all of his dreams of winning a contest at the Pendleton Roundup. It took more than one wing to ride a bull, ride a bareback horse, rope a calf, bulldog a steer, and many other feats that was open to the contestants. The drunken cowboy was holding his hand above his head, screaming bloody murder as the knife was protruding from his wrist. It would be a long time before that wrist saw much action again; that seemed to sober up his other four comrades as they asked the bartender to send someone for the doctor. The sheriff was called, and statements were taken from everyone who saw the fight. Will, Jack, and I was exonerated from any wrongdoing. The word of the fight and my knife-throwing was spreading like a range fire over the prairie. After retrieving my knife, we three went up to our rooms an undressed for a good night's sleep.

Next morning, at the breakfast table in the hotel, a reporter walked over to our table and said, "Gentlemen, may I please have a word with you three?"

"Of course," we said, "always happy to talk to the press."

He questioned us about the donnybrook last night in the saloon about the fact that the drunken cowboy was pulling his weapon during the fight and I was throwing my knife accurately into his wrist. I told the reporter that they, the cowboys, were drunk; his mind was in a foggy shambles; and I didn't want to kill him but I couldn't stand by and see him shoot my friend Jack Sundown; so I did the next best thing the circumstances called for. At least I thought it was the best thing to disable him from pulling the trigger. That was all I did.

The reporter said, "Are you three the same three that solved the sex slave ring in Portland a few weeks ago?"

We said, "Yes, we are."

He asked if we were also the cowboys that rounded up the rustling ring here in Fossil.

We nodded yes.

He said, "You are also the cowboys that stopped the train robbery of the Old Minnesota Railroad in Weiser, Idaho?"

Again, we nodded yes.

He then asked if the three of us had any plans for the future.

We said, "The only immediate plan we have is going to the Pendleton Roundup Rodeo and watching my first cousin, Bobby Chestnut, and this gentleman here, Jack Sundown, exercise their right to perform in the contests there."

The reporter then asked if we were not working for the Double O Bar Ranch.

We said, "No, we're not."

He wanted to know why.

I told him, "Tom O'Brien and I have a difference of opinion— my relationship with his daughter, Patricia—and he told me to leave. Will and Jack left the ranch with me."

The reporter said, "Do I have your permission to print this story?"

The three of us said, "Yes, it's all true."

The reporter went to his office and started writing his column. It started,

Once again the local modern-day Sherlock Holmes has raised his head to foil another callous deed here in Fossil. After being fired from the Double O Bar Ranch and riding seventy miles into Fossil, he and his partners were accosted in the Star saloon by five drunken cowboys on their way to the Pendleton Roundup. They evidently recognized Jack Sundown as a past and current contestant at the Pendleton Roundup. Jack Sundance was called several derogatory names, and a fight ensued. It was five cowboys against three cowboys. It was an even fight until one of the drunken cowboys pulled his gun. Bill Chestnut, the modern-day Sherlock Holmes, drew his knife from his belt sheath and threw it into the cowboy's wrist, which was pulling his weapon, therefore saving the life of Jack Sundown. They are on their way tomorrow to the Pendleton Roundup, where Bill Chestnut's first cousin, Bobby, is performing. Jack Sundown is also performing at the rodeo. If you remember sometime back, our newspaper did an article on these three—William Chestnut, Jack Sundown, and their friend, Will—telling our readers of these three men's escapades. In the last year and a half they stopped a train robbery, saved the payroll, arrested what bandits were left after the shoot-up, rounded up a group of rustlers in this local vicinity, arrested three horse thieves, and were instrumental in capturing a gang selling stolen women as sex slaves in Portland. These men can be trusted, and they would be someone to ride the river with. As of now, they are at loose ends looking for a job, after the rodeo is over. In my opinion, these three men are worthy of the name *cowboy*.

This column was picked up by most of the Western newspapers and reprinted. Bobby and the O'Brien family also read the article that was reprinted in the Pendleton newspaper.

The next day, we three and Major continued our journey to Pendleton, Oregon, and then on to the rodeo grounds where we met Bobby and some of the other ranch hands. Bobby was really excited about the news article that the O'Brien family had read. He wanted to know all the details and thanked me for saving Jack's life, as they are close friends. We saw Thomas O'Brien approaching our group, and I excused myself and went over to another part of the rodeo grounds where they were making up a stagecoach run around the arena, showing the crowd what a stagecoach robbery looked like under an Indian attack. There were a few real Indians in the group that were going to attack the stagecoach, but most were cowboys wearing Indian garb.

The attack on the stagecoach was to be enacted the next morning as the first attraction. Bobby was going to be the stagecoach driver, and he knew how to handle the six up horses pulling the stagecoach, very well. The three of us spent the rest of the day walking around the rodeo grounds, checking on the wild bulls, horses that were in the bareback contest, talking to the other contestants, and generally trying to learn the ins and outs of the rodeo game. Most of the contestants knew Bobby. They had seen his performances over the past few years, and they wished him luck. Before stopping at the rodeo grounds, we had taken a room at one of the lesser hotels inasmuch as the better hotels had been reserved sometime ahead, but at least it was close to the rodeo grounds.

We had supper at a greasy spoon across the street from the saloon, and after eating, we walked over to the saloon for a nightcap.

The same five cowboys that we had the encounter in Fossil were in the saloon. The cowboy that had vilified Jack—his hand bandaged and his arm in a sling—was there. This time they were almost sober, and the one that I stuck with the knife got up from the table and walked over to us.

He said, "I want no trouble. I just wanted to come over and apologize to you, Jack, for my unruly manner. I meant no disrespect for you or your heritage. I just had more rotgut than I could handle."

Jack said, "I accept your apology, no hard feelings. Sorry about your hand."

The cowboy said, "I deserved that for pulling my gun. I know I could have been dead instead."

He walked back to his friends' table.

We all decided it was time to hit our bunks; tomorrow would be a busy day. We would be up early for the rodeo. Little did I know how busy it was really going to be.

Next morning, after eating at the greasy spoon for breakfast, I had three pancakes with an egg between each pancake with maple syrup and bacon. The menu called it saddle blankets. We drifted over to the rodeo grounds, where the contestants were preparing for the stagecoach race. They were putting on their Indian garb and putting harness on the horses. Bobby was checking the stagecoach out from top to bottom, stem to stern, and all were loading their pistols and rifles with "blank ammunition." All that was in the brass was powder, and the wadding paper needed to keep the powder inside the brass. Jack was already in his buckskins, and he cut a handsome figure. It was surprising how much hustle and bustle and work it took put on a show for the spectators.

The crowd had gathered for the stagecoach run; the bleachers were full; cotton candy, beer, and other drinks were prevalent. Everyone seemed to be having a wonderful time. The two rear doors of the arena burst open, and out came six beautifully matched horses pulling a Wells Fargo stage. Bobby was on the seat holding the reins, and in behind the coach came the howling Indians shooting their weapons. All with the supposedly blank bullets about halfway down the arena, Bobby stood up and toppled off the stagecoach seat, hitting the ground solidly. We all rushed over to him, and blood was running out from under his garments. To our horror, it was apparent that Bobby had been shot. They had a doctor on the rodeo grounds in case of emergencies, and he ran over with his medical bag and examined Bobby and told us that he had been shot in the back close to his back bone and that he was in very serious condition. He must be taken to the doctor's emergency room for an immediate operation. He was losing blood rapidly. I was horrified that someone could do so dastardly a deed.

Will, Jack, Mr. O'Brien, and I helped take Bobby on a gurney to the doctor's office and to his operating room. His nurse was there ready to help. The doctor was barking out orders to her and everyone else in the vicinity on what to do to stop Bobby's flow of vital blood.

Bobby was in and out consciousness, and when he was conscious, we could barely hear him saying, "Bill, help me," over and over, saying the same thing but getting weaker each time.

The doctor said, "He has lost too much blood for him to operate. He needs a blood transfusion. We must find a donor."

I told the doctor that I was his first cousin. "Check my blood and see if it would match, and I would give him the transfusion."

Thank God, it did match. I lay down beside Bobby, praying that my blood would save his life.

From my bunk next to Bobby, I told Jack and Will, "Go to the sheriff and the rodeo grounds, get all the pistols and rifles that had been used in the stagecoach run, get the list of names of each person that had been assigned a pistol or carbine, keep the pistols and carbines safe until I am able to examine each of them individually and carefully. We can't wait, the evidence may be destroyed. I am going to find the bastard that shot Bobby in the back."

Lying on the bunk beside Bobby, I could feel the beat of my heart pumping frantically. I could feel my life giving blood rush from my body into Bobby's—the feeling of helping or maybe saving someone you love. He was my only kin; it was an awesome feeling and responsibility that not many people experienced. The operation was taking longer than was anticipated. The bullet was lodged on the base of his rib, where it was attached to his spine, and it was a delicate operation so close to his spine. One slip of the scalpel could sever his spinal cord. I could feel myself getting weaker as the blood was being pumped out of my body into Bobby, but I was glad that I had enough blood in my system to serve Bobby's needs. I was half asleep due to low blood in my own body when the doctor shook me and said the operation was over and Bobby, although in critical condition, had a good chance of recovery. He assigned his nurse to give me the proper nourishment to rebuild my blood supply and recover, which would take several hours.

When I awoke, I was feeling refreshed from the food that the nurse had given me. I felt my strength had returned. Although I was still a little weak in the knees, I could maneuver okay. My first duty. I felt, was go to the ranch because Bobby was still the foreman, and although I had been fired, I knew the ranch needed a foreman, so I told Jack if it was all right with O'Brien, that he, Jack, should take Bobby's place on the ranch until Bobby had recovered. If Jack wanted to come with me, then he could find Will and my location and come then. In the meantime, I suggested to Jack that he pick up all of Bobby's contests and show whoever had shot Bobby that Jack was as good as Bobby and deny them their victory at the rodeo. Bobby would like that as well as me. All the weapons had been handed over to the sheriff. He had them locked in his office for our perusal. It was time to find the culprit. I had a hunch that one of the drunken cowboys that we had encountered in the Star saloon in Fossil was behind the attempted murder of Bobby. I asked the sheriff to get all five names. I wanted to match them to the list of the participants who were in the group that was supposed to be shooting blanks at the stagecoach.

The doctor had taken out of Bobby's back a 4440 slug. It was a little misshapen from hitting Bobby's rib. That's when the doctor weighed the bullet. It was assuredly a 4440. We looked at all the 4440 weapons in the sheriff's office and lay them to one side. I asked the sheriff if he had a cleaning patch designed to clean the barrel of a 4440 and if so, bring it to the table. I assumed that there would be much more powder residue in the barrel that held the blank cartridge than in the barrel of the gun that had a real bullet coming out of the barrel; the projectile would push a lot of the spent powder out of the barrel when it was fired. I told the sheriff, Will, and Jack my theory, and they agreed it was likely so. We used the list of all the cowboys that had taken a 4440 weapon from the quartermaster of the rodeo and matched them with the weapons. Sure enough, one of the cowboys from the Star saloon in Fossil had the least amount of powder residue in the barrel and had signed out the 4440.

"He's our man," I said.

The sheriff was convinced that the evidence we found would hold up in front of the circuit judge, but we wanted to question him at great length to find out whose idea it was. The sheriff arrested all five men and put them in separate cells. We wanted to question them separately and use a little reverse psychology, trying to get each of them to admit to their knowledge of the terrible deed. We used the good cop–bad cop routine. Jack was the good cop, and I was the bad cop; and believe me, I was going to be the bad cop.

I said, "Jack, remember in Portland, when I questioned the sex slave traders. I want you and Will and the sheriff to look the other way, and I don't want the other four men to see my prisoner, just hear him when he hollers."

And they would hear him when he hollered if he didn't come clean quickly. I had my prisoner handcuffed with his hands behind his back, and he could hardly move a muscle.

I said, "Let's have a talk before we get into this serious questioning. You have shot my only living relative, someone I think very highly of. As far as you are concerned, you are only helpful to me if you talk. If you don't talk, I have no use for you at all, and I will make you suffer like you've never suffered before with the expertise of my knife. My knife is designed for me to throw and hit my target as you saw in the Star saloon, but it will do many more services in the hands of an artist like me. I don't want to give you any false pretense of sympathy, because I have none for you. When you don't answer my question truthfully or not at all, I shall use my knife to remove your fingernails one at a time. Each question unanswered truthfully, well, there goes another nail. After I have removed all ten of your fingers and thumbnails, I'll start on your feet. But I believe the pain will be so excruciating that you will answer my questions before we get that far. Now, shall we begin? Who told you to shoot and kill Bobby?"

The prisoner answered, "The foreman of the ranch."

"Were the other four men also implicated in Bobby's shooting?"

"Yes," he said.

"Was the owner of the ranch implicated in the shooting?"

He said, "I don't know for sure."

I told the prisoner that he was doing very good but I was a little unhappy. I wasn't able to carve on your fingers yet.

I said, "How much did the foreman pay you?"

He said, "$500 total."

I said, "Not much money for a man's life."

I called the sheriff, Jack, and Will to the cell and told them what my prisoner had said. I requested that the sheriff get a pen and paper and write down his confession and have him sign it even with an *X* if necessary, witnessed by each of us, implicating the other four men and the foreman of the Rafter Ranch. With a little more interrogation of the four and getting a written statement from the foreman, we might be able to implicate the owner of the ranch, and in my opinion, he was as guilty as the perpetrators. Somehow, the confessions were leaked from the jail, and the word spread that we had arrested the attempted murderers of Bobby Chestnut. Crowds were forming outside the jail, and many of them had whiskey bottles in their hands, and some of them had coiled ropes over their shoulders. It didn't look good for the prisoners. The spectators remembered Bobby Chestnut from previous rodeos, and they were all mad as hell. The sheriff of Pendleton, Oregon, sent a telegram to the sheriff of Fossil and told him to go get the owner of the Rafter ranch and hold him for questioning, as long as he could, also the foreman.

Men rioting in the Main Street were getting angrier as time passed. They were yelling for the sheriff to turn over the prisoners. They wanted to have a five-men hanging party and make this Pendleton Roundup one to remember. The sheriff persisted that these five men and perhaps a few others would be tried for attempted murder. And if Bobby died, they would hang legitimately.

"So go home and sleep it off."

It was a surly crowd. Most of them were out of state or out of towners, and that's probably what saved the sheriff from having a lynching on his hands.

Information about what had happened to Bobby and what the sheriff had to say at the press conference was told. He requested that Jack, Will, and I be at the conference. The same reporter that reported the Star saloon incident a few days back was also there, taking in the rodeo. He looked at the three of us and said, "Here we go again."

The sheriff told the reporters what we had accomplished in apprehending the attempted murderers. He told them what my plan was in the very beginning and how I brought it into action. That everything was my idea and he saw the simplicity of the plan and went along completely. He told the reporters that we had signed confessions from the entire five men. There was no doubt about their guilt and collusion in the active attempted murder case. Again the deductions of the local modern-day Sherlock Holmes (Alias William Chestnut) had struck again, finding the criminals at an astounding fast pace. His powers of deduction seem unusual. There were plenty of newspaper reporters at the rodeo, and they were clamoring for unlimited access to us. It was a huge story in the Western United States newspapers. It seems like the three of us are celebrities again. Next day, after the newspaper article was reprinted, we started receiving telegrams from old and new friends alike. We never knew we had that many friends until now.

The rodeo was over. Jack had excelled in all of his contests, the ranch's reputation was saved, and it was time to return to the ranch. Bobby was still in critical condition and could not be moved until he was more thoroughly recovered. I stayed with Bobby until he was recovered enough to make the journey back to the ranch by himself. Will and I did not want to go back to the ranch, as it would only be more difficult for Patricia and I the second time we had to part. We kept receiving telegrams of congratulations on apprehending the potential murderers, and we did get to meet the owner of the Rafter ranch and interrogate him on his part in the attempted murder. We had the foreman in jail in Fossil, with a signed confession, implicating the owner of the Rafter ranch—who was also in jail in Fossil. The five men were in jail in Pendleton. It looked like a clean sweep. The sheriff insisted that we three—Jack, Will, and I—remain in Pendleton until the circuit court convened. He said our testimony, even though we had a signed confession on everyone except the ranch owner and we could solidify the attempted murder case, we gave our testimony live in front of the circuit judge. Luckily, Will and I had the funds to carry us over until the court convened. Jack was still in the employment of the Double Bar Ranch, so his expenses were borne by the ranch.

During the waiting period for Bobby's recovery and the time when the circuit court judge made his rounds, we had gotten several interesting offers for employment. The columns in the newspapers had spread our name—and fame, if you want to call it that—over the Western United States; and fortunately or unfortunately, our name was almost a household word. I was hoping that I would see Patricia sometime doing the trial and we could spend some quality time with each other, discussing our future and some of the job offers I had received. Her acquiescence was very important to the job that I would ultimately choose.

I had talked to Will about the offers, and he said, "Bill, I'm open to go with you on any job that you choose for us, and I'm sure Jack feels the same."

The time for the trial was fast approaching. Word had it that the circuit court judge would be here in about one week. They were readying the courthouse, adding additional chairs and furnishings, as it was expected to be a very large audience during this astounding trial. The word was out, and a lot of the local dignitaries and some dignitaries from out of state were going to be on hand to listen to all the testimony at this trial. The prisoners from the jail in Fossil, the owner of Rafter bar, and his foreman would be brought to Pendleton for trial. Five of the men were still in the jail in Pendleton being held for the trial.

I was anxious for the trial to begin inasmuch as I wanted to see Patricia and talk to her about our plans. I didn't know for sure that Mr. O'Brien would bring his family to the trial, but as it was, his foreman of the ranch that got shot, I believed he had at least a duty to come to the trial, and I was hoping he'd bring Patricia with him. Also Jack and Bobby would be coming from the ranch to testify at the trial. I wanted to talk to Jack about some of the job offers that Will and I had been discussing. One job in particular that came from the Old Minnesota Railroad sounded as if it could work out for all three of us. I didn't realize how huge the railroad conglomerate was and all the other great businesses. They owned lumber companies, citrus farms, ranches, steamship lines. I could go on and on, but they were huge holdings. The president wanted to talk to the three of us about becoming railroad detectives. It sounded like it could be an exciting job. We would be traveling over the United States, correcting the atrocities that mankind did to each other. The job sounds like it would be much diversified, which would suit all of our talents; and as far as I could figure out, the pay would be good, which we would discuss when meeting the president and CEO of the railroad. It would mean that my access to seeing Patricia would be curtailed, but I would make every effort to see her when I could, and I would write her often. Will liked the sound of the job, and I was hoping that Jack would like it. Also, we would have access to almost all railroad lines free of charge. They had a reciprocal agreement, which was honored by all railroads. We'd have a personal boxcar for our horses and gear to travel with us at all times, and of course, don't forget Major; he was one of the crew.

The day of the trial was here. The city of Pendleton was filling up to the brim with spectators from all over the Western United States. I had received word from the president of the Old Great Minnesota railroad (James J. Hill) that he would be in town in a special Pullman car on the side rail for the length of the trial. I believed he was here to check on Will, Jack, and I to see what kind of men we were before he committed to our hiring. No one could blame an employer for checking out his potential employees. We were informed of his arrival and his request to have a private dinner with us three in his private car. Jack had been back to Pendleton for only one day, but we tried to fill him in on all known details. So he knew most of the offers before the dinner engagement. At least Jack knew all we knew.

We notified the president of the railroad that we could not have dinner with him that evening, as it was the beginning of the trial, and we would be called upon to testify. It was our sworn duty to tell all we knew to the judge and jury, and believe me, we weren't going to leave anything out of the testimony. We each had our say and were excused from further testimony. Then the hard evidence was given—the signed confessions, the signing of the quartermaster records, for the use of the 4440, the stipulations that was given as to the powder residue left in the barrel, the doctor's testimony of the wound, and the bullet that was found embedded in Bobby's rib near his backbone, the transfusion, the doctor using my blood to pull Bobby through, the confession of the Rafter foreman implicating the owner of the Rafter Ranch. The evidence was overwhelming. It took the jury thirty minutes to deliberate, and to a person, they all were found guilty as charged. The judge said he would take a couple of days to deliberate the punishment for all seven men.

The newspaper across the entire front page in bold letters said,

All Found Guilty

Due to the excellent detective work by Bill Chestnut and his friends, these vile men were found guilty and awaiting sentencing by the circuit judge. We hope the judge gives a long hard sentence to the attempted murders. Nothing can be hard enough for their actions.

As said before, if you listen to the devil's music, you must pay the fiddler.

I had tried often since the O'Brien family had gotten to Pendleton for the trial to see Patricia and finally found her in a dressmaker's shop in downtown Pendleton. Someone had told me where she was. I couldn't remember who, but I went there as fast as possible to see her before she left the shop. I told her I had been searching for her ever since she had gotten into town but had been unsuccessful; evidently, her father had been keeping her away from any location that I would be visiting. She told me that she had been beside herself trying to find me and wishing with all her heart that we could be together; even for a short time would be better than no time at all.

We hugged each other strongly and lusciously. When we felt each other in our arms, peace filled our being. Tears came to Patricia's eyes, and I had difficulty keeping the tears out of my own. Our feelings for each other were like the great writer Shakespeare had talked about in Romeo and Juliet, although I hoped our ending would be better.

She told me that her father was sending her back east to Boston to a lady's finishing school. She didn't tell me the name of the school. She had not learned it yet but would notify me the first chance that she had. It was a two-year school, and she was not looking forward to being gone away from me for that long. I told her I had an appointment to see the president of the Old Great Minnesota Railroad. He was here in Pendleton on a side rail in his Pullman car and had invited Will, Jack, and me to dinner to discuss a job.

"I don't know if he even would hire us or what the job might be, but I will make every attempt to see you in Boston. This is probably your father's way to keep us apart and let both of us mature a few years to be sure that we love each other enough to overcome these adversities. With your permission, Patricia, I will probably take the railroad job if offered, until we become of age to make our own decisions. I don't understand what your father has against me. I have torn myself apart mentally looking for his flaw in myself but found none. I'll write you and Bobby telling you of my job and whereabouts whenever I can. Until then, remember our pledge to each other, and I will do the same."

I contacted the president of the railroad and told him, if it was okay with him and his staff, we could meet with him for dinner tomorrow night. The trial was over, and we could not have left any stone unturned to convict these attempted murderers. We had heard the scuttlebutt that the circuit judge had pronounced sentence on all seven men—giving twenty years at hard labor with no chance of parole, a fitting sentence for their atrocities.

The dinner date was agreed. The three of us put on our best, cleanest dirty clothes that we had for the dinner. The master chef outdid himself. It was the best dinner that the three of us had ever eaten. Some of the food were French cooking, and I could not even pronounce the name, but it was still marvelous.

The president said, "I have been looking a long time for three such as you, whom I can trust and who has the intelligence to carry out tough assignments, and what I have read and what I have seen at the trial, you are those three men."

He told us that the railroad holdings were all over the United States, and in this work, which would require a lot of traveling, we would do a lot of detective work and be in serious danger. The assignments that he would give to us would be of great importance, greater than he would give to ordinary men. He felt that we were cut from a different cloth, and we could handle most circumstances. He told us that we would be free under our own orders except for the assignments given to us by him. We could handle each situation as we saw fit. We could call upon the resources of the railroad at anytime to handle any special problems.

"You will answer only to me, not my subordinates. I want to reiterate, only to me. I'm sure we can agree on your pay, which I will lavishly pay you. Only I can fire you. I will give you identification that no one can repute. My first job for you three will be to go to my very large ranch in northwest Texas on the Llano Estacado, known as the Staked Plains. It's by the Canadian River. I have been having a lot of trouble with rustlers, and I know you three have had that kind of problems before. If you decide to work for me, that will be your first assignment, locate and destroy the rustlers. I'll give you my foreman's name and the ranch manager's name. I also have here the ranch manager's last report for the three of you to examine. You can come with your own conclusions."

"Mr. President, you have hired yourself three loyal cowboys, we will work for the brand. We will each need identification letters showing that we work for the railroad. So if one of us get misplaced or shot or dead, the other two will still have the identification needed to continue our assignment. You can trust us as we'll trust you. No word of this employment should reach beyond this car."

"Done," said the President. "I'll contact you men discreetly with all the necessary paperwork in the next few days, your pay starts now."

We discussed, the three of us, the railroad president's dinner and the job offer after we had gotten back to our hotel. It seemed as if we were in accord; this was probably the best job we could get and reaffirmed our determination to do a good job. We could tell from our discussion with the president that the perks were going to be outstanding, with a lot of assignments and travel. It would be an interesting time in our lives, if we live long enough to enjoy it. I knew that we three could and would carry our own weight. Will and I were excellent shots. Jack could hit what he shoots at, but he wasn't as fast as Will and I. But he had the unique ability to use the primitive bow and arrow when needed and the ability to read sign better than either Will or me, so the three of us will make a good team, and of course, there's Major.

A few days later, by private courier, we received the paperwork needed for our assignment. It had the paperwork for each of us granting us the authority that he had offered and we had suggested. Now was the time to get started doing our job. He had also sent some cash vouchers to us for our traveling expenses. We gathered up all our gear that we possessed got our animals, took them down to the railroad yard, talked to the person in charge, reserved a boxcar for our horses and gear, and got tickets for the town of Tuscarora also Mobeetie, Texas. These were the nearest towns to the ranch. Our plan was that Will would get off the train at Tuscarora, Jack would get off the train at Mobeetie, and I would get off at Clarendon, Texas. We did not want to be seen together, and each of us would arrive at the ranch at different times and different directions. We wanted no one to know that we were the three musketeers, so to speak. We would all try and get hired on at the ranch in our own ways. We didn't want to alert the foreman or the manager at this point in the investigation. Rustlers come in all disguises, and they might be in disguise. We also agreed to fictitious names they might have read the newspapers or heard about our exploits by word-of-mouth, so we could take no chances. Before we had left Pendleton, Oregon, I had the saddlemaker sew a waterproof pocket under the skirt of our saddles where we would carry our identification papers; we wanted no one to know we're agents of the railroad. We'd keep the papers hidden and dry; we didn't know the trail ahead and what it might bring. We had to change railroads a few times to reach our destination, but we agreed that this was the best way to travel for our purposes. Our horses were fresh when we disembarked at our assigned locations. We had cashed some railroad vouchers, giving us the cash we needed for our performances, and we were on the ground of our assignment. Just how we were going to complete our duty was still up in the air. It seemed that if you want to meet some unruly men, you congregated at the local watering hole or saloon. We each had said our goodbyes to each other and looked forward to our meeting at the ranch; we were on our own.

After securing a hotel room, I drifted over to the local watering hole to start my investigation. I walked through the bat wing doors of the saloon over to the bar and asked the bartender, who was bald-headed and big as a horse, if he had some coffee. Several of the cowboys sitting at the tables looked around to see who ordered coffee in a saloon. There was a large painting over the bar of a nude woman, and all she had on was a scarf over the lower part of her body hiding the imaginative part.

I hung around the saloon for a few days, letting the patrons and the bartender get used to my being there. I asked the bartender, who was always a wonderful source of information, if he knew of any ranches in the general vicinity looking for hands.

He said, "Put your name up on the chalkboard, and the type of work you're looking for and what you have done in the past, the foreman of the ranches in the area come here twice a week looking for hands, and maybe one of them will hire you. I said, "I sure hope so."

I was getting short on funds. I had noticed some cowboys coming into the saloon at various times, and I had willingly talked to them and bought them a few drinks, saying, "I am surely looking for a job and I'm not too particular, as to what I do. I need a place to quietly get lost for a while. I was giving information as if I might be on the dodge. A couple of the cowboys worked on the ranch owned by the railroad. About a week later, the foreman of the ranch in question and the two cowboys came to the saloon. He saw my name on the chalkboard and walked over to my table.

He said, "I assume by your name being on the chalkboard you're looking for a job?"

I said, "Yes, I am in need a job real bad, and I'm not too particular as to what kind of job it may be."

He asked me a few questions, and then he got down to what I believe was the basics.

He said, "Can you shoot a pistol?"

I said, "Some."

He said, "Let's go out on the edge of town and see just how good you are."

I asked, "Are you going to be my competition, or are you going to put that on one of your cowboys? When I pull my iron, I mean business, it's not just for a demonstration or fun."

The foreman said, "Sam here is one of my better gun handlers. I'll let him take you on."

I said, "Mr. Foreman, Sam and whatever the other cowboy's name may be is not good enough to take me on."

He seemed a little agitated at my bravado, but I assured him it was true. I told him I didn't want to kill out of hand and if we could use some other inanimate object. I didn't want to kill his cowboys.

He said, rather smugly, "We'll find something."

I said, "That's fine with me, I'll leave it up to you."

As we were riding at the edge of town, the foreman saw a building. Actually, it was an old livery stable that had two weather vanes on top of the building. It was unoccupied and had weathered lumber and was in need of desperate repair. He stopped his horse in the middle of the dusty street and looked at the weather vanes, looked at me, and looked at his men.

He said, "Here's our target." He told his fast gun to see if he could pull and hit the target. The weather vanes were in fairly decent condition, and they would twirl in the wind, and they made a screeching noise, which could be very irritating to people in the vicinity. We tied our horses to the hitch rail out front of the building and walked to the center of the street, and each step that we took, a puff of dust would cloud up around our legs. It was very dusty in this part of Texas as the total rainfall averaged around twenty inches a year, and with the town's activity on the only street, the dirt was always ground to find dust. The foreman asked me if I could draw and hit the two weather vanes were painted roosters, which could use some touch up.

I said, "Say the word, and I'll give you an unwanted demonstration of my gun skills."

He told his fast gun to draw and hit the weathervane. To me, it seemed that he drew moderately fast, and he did hit the weathervane.

The foreman said, "Can you beat that?"

Without answering, I pulled my .45 rapidly and shot the same weathervane three times and kept it going around and around, shooting off the roosters head with the last round. I whirled and shot the second weathervane with my remaining three shots, hitting it and making it go round and round and round until it slowed and stopped the last round. I had shot off the roosters' head like before, so they knew the first time was no accident. None of the three men spoke; my actions spoke louder than words. They had never seen a demonstration of shooting skill like that. Inasmuch as I had emptied my gun, shooting the weather vanes, the other cowboy decided he would draw on me. As his hand reached for his pistol, I threw my knife that I kept under the collar of my shirt, hitting him in his forearm, and he dropped his weapon. The move with my knife was so fast it caught all three cowboys by complete surprise.

The foreman looked at me and said, "You're full of surprises."

I said, "Some, you haven't seen it all yet."

He said, "As of today you're hired, your pay is one and a half dollars a day and found."

I said, "That sounds fine to me, but I'm out of funds now, I would like to have a small advance."

He reached in his vest pocket and pulled out two $20 gold pieces and said, "This is advance on your pay, now let's get to the ranch."

We took the cowboy with the forearm wound to the doctor and had it sewed up, disinfected, wrapped. We were on our way to the ranch, and I was wondering if Will or Jack had made it to the ranch also. If not, I was compelled to go it alone. Of course, I couldn't leave Will and Jack hanging out. I would have to go find them if they didn't show. But I still have a job to do, and I had to do it discreetly.

I was introduced to the ranch manager and was told that I would start work tomorrow.

"Go pick out your bunk in the bunkhouse, stable your Appaloosa mare (which they all admired), and introduce yourself to the cookie"—in other words make myself at home.

I had Major with me, which they all accepted. The crew that was on the ranch seemed to be a salty bunch, and I believed they would take no guff from anyone. They had a young kid hired to more or less take care of the bunkhouse, clean the floors, be sure they had water for drinking and washing—in general be the maintenance man for the bunkhouse. He was a go-and-fetch man for all the crew. I had to play my cards close to the vest, because I was wading into deep water, and if I wasn't careful, I could drown. I think you know what I mean.

There were a total of about twenty-five men in this crew. I was sure not all of them or perhaps any of them are rustlers, but it was my job to ferret out the guilty. I was told by some of the cowboys that the ranch carried about one hundred thousand head of cattle; some were mother cows, and some were steers being readied for the market. The crew knew that this ranch was owned by a very large conglomerate railroad; they didn't have quite the loyalty to the brand as if the owner had been an individual, but they were being paid, and they would do the job. The code of the "cowboy "prevails. They all seemed to know that the ranch cattle were being rustled. But they didn't know who or how. At least they wouldn't spill the beans on their cohorts.

Several days passed, and still no Will or Jack appeared. I was getting worried that something could have happened to them. I was in no position to go look for them. At this time, I had to play my hand as dealt. As I was riding the fence one afternoon, I saw and smelled smoke, and I was inquisitive as who would be out in the open-range building a fire with enough Greenwood to make smoke. Major and I cautiously went in the direction that the smoke was coming from. The wind was blowing from the east, and the smell was very distinctive. I used Major and what skills he had and tried to creep up on the campfire. As we approached the fire, no one seemed to be in the vicinity, until we got within perhaps one hundred yards of the fire and someone behind us said, "Stick up your hands," and we complied.

I said *we*—Major stopped when I stopped, and I put up my hands.

A gruff voice said, "Don't turn around, or I'll shoot."

I continued standing still with my hands up in the air, feeling a little foolish but cautious. I could hear the crunch of the gravel beneath his boot soles, and it was becoming louder, and I knew he was approaching us from the rear. I looked at Major, and he had been looking backward, and his tail started wagging, and I thought to myself that he must know who this individual was. So I thought I would take a chance and make a quick turn but be ready to pull my iron as fast as I ever did, and what I saw was Jack Sundown walking toward me, laughing hard but silently. I gave him a few choice words out of my repertoire, which only made him laugh more. We gave each other a manly hug, saying how good it was to see each other. I asked about Will, and he said he knew nothing; he hadn't seen or heard of Will since he left the train.

I told Jack all of my endeavors up to this point, about being hired by the foreman of the ranch, about him wanting to see my shooting skills, and that I had hinted that I would be open perhaps to a little skullduggery if the occasion arose. I told him that I believed that the foreman had something to do with the cattle's disappearance. That I had met the manager of the ranch as well, and I was still holding my own opinion about his involvement in the cattle disappearance. Jack told me he had been riding around in the greater vicinity of the ranch by himself, keeping his own visual to see what he could learn. He said that he had seen cattle-truck tracks and a lot of cattle tracks. It looked to him that the cattle was being transported in the cattle trucks—where, he didn't know; how many was taken, he could only guess. But they were a lot of cattle tracks around and a few horse tracks. One of the horse tracks had an odd weight on one side of the shoe that the furrier was probably trying to straighten out the hoof and was using the horseshoe method. It would be easily recognizable.

"Here, Bill," said Jack, "let me draw you a picture of the horse-shoe, and he did."

We talked till late evening, trying to figure out what was happening with the cattle. We believed that some of the crew were herding the cattle to a prearranged location and were met by the cattle trucks and taken to the buyer's location. This is a fast method to move a lot of cattle, with very little chance of detection. You could strip a range quickly of cattle with this type of operation.

I'd go back to the ranch and see if I could locate the horse with the telltale horseshoe and find out who the rider was. Jack would stay out on the range, seeing if he could pick up more important sign. I gave Jack all the provisions I had in my saddlebags; I could get more later. Most important to Jack was the Arbuckle coffee grounds that I carried around. The horse with the corrective shoe was easy to spot out in the remunda. His owner was a big burly cowboy who had been on the ranch three years, by the name of Mike. I didn't know Mike but I'd try to find out more about him and his habits. I was still concerned about Will. I hadn't heard from him, and I was getting worried. He was my oldest friend since I left the farm several years ago. We had traveled a lot of rough roads together, and I must take the risk of finding him. I knew he was capable of taking care of himself, but each of us in our lives got in a pinch, and we needed someone's help. I'd do what I can. I asked the foreman if I could take a week off to take care of some unfinished business that I had before I came to the ranch. He said yes, but I thought he was a little suspicious, so I had to be extra careful in my search for Will. I thought the foreman didn't want to lose my gun or knife talents.

I saddled my Appaloosa mare and headed for Tuscarora, Texas, where Will had gotten off the train. I had a few dollars in my pocket, so I wasn't too worried about getting along. I was more worried about Will than anything else at this time. I thought that maybe I would go find Jack out on the range and tell him what I intended to do. I wanted to keep him informed as to my whereabouts. I went to the general vicinity where I had seen Jack last and looked for sign. Major had his nose to the ground, and the way he was acting, I believed he picked up Jack's scent, so I followed him; and sure enough, after an hour or so, Major located Jack around a campsite. We palavered some, and I told Jack about finding the matching horseshoe print. I told Jack that I had taken off a week from the ranch work. I told the foreman that I had some unfinished business to take care of for about a week. He gave me permission. I told Jack I was heading for Tuscarora's to find out any information I could as to Wills whereabouts. He wanted to go along, but I suggested that he stay out on the range like he'd been doing in case there was another cattle run and he might get some additional information.

"I would be back in a week or sooner if I can find Will. If not, I may stay gone for ten days or so, I must have some inkling as to Wills whereabouts."

It took too hard days and hard riding to reach Tuscarora. I was sure ready for a little comfort, but I was anxious to find out what I could about Will. I went to the livery and got a stall for my horse, told the livery man to clean her up wash her down, curry, and feed her some grain and good hay. She had earned it these last two days. I then went to the hotel and got a room, stowed my gear, and ambled over to the saloon were you could get most information you're looking for. This was a typical saloon with a picture of a seminude woman over the bar, as most of these rowdy towns have. I talked to the bartender, asked for a cup of coffee, told him I had been riding on the trail for some time, and had run out of Arbuckle coffee and needed a cup badly. He was sympathetic and brought me a cup right away. I then told him I was looking for a friend that had gotten into town a week or so earlier by train, and I was supposed to meet him here and wondered if he had seen him. I described Will and to him as best I could, not having a tintype to show him.

He said, "I believe I saw him here three or four days ago, but I haven't seen him since."

I asked him, "Was anyone else with him?"

And he said, "He was talking to a truck driver who hauls cattle."

My ears perked up. I asked the bartender if he knew whom these truckers worked for, and he said, "I believe it's the Smith Cattle Holding Company. They have a garage across town."

I thanked the bartender for his information and said, "I'll be back soon, see you later." I walked out the saloon door and looked down the street three or four doors and saw the sheriff's office.

I decided I would go and talk to the sheriff and get what information I could from him without revealing my or Will's connection to the railroad. I gave the same description to the sheriff that I had given to the bartender, but not a name, as I really didn't know what name Will was using here in Tuscarora. The sheriff recognized the description that I had given him and confirmed that he was working for the cattle holding company. I couldn't go to the cattle holding company and ask for John Doe, so I had to locate the garage and spend what time was necessary waiting for Will to appear to catch his eye so we could discuss the information I and Jack had gathered and what information he had gathered working for the cattle holding company. Off and on, it was a two-day wait.

Will showed up with two other tough guys in the same truck. I rode my Appaloosa mare down the street in front of the cattle company's headquarters, so Will could not help but notice me. He didn't let on that we knew each other. I continued farther down the street to the saloon, tied my horse to the hitch rail, went in through the bat wing doors, and got a corner table. This time I didn't want to arouse suspicion. So instead of coffee, I ordered a glass of beer to suck on slowly until I knew Will would be arriving.

Other workers came into the saloon; some stood at the bar. Some got a table, but no Will. I knew Will enough that something was up. I knew Will would be anxious to see and talk to me, but something or someone was keeping him from the saloon. I didn't know if they had caught on to his identity or his purpose or if they were being overly cautious because he was a new man and would not let him out on his own accord. This was going to be a touchy moment, trying to get Will by himself. I believed that the two men who were with Will in the cab of the truck when he returned to the cattle company's office came in to the saloon. They haphazardly sat down at a table next to me, and I could hear the conversation, although it was in a subdued tone. They were saying that the new hand was working out okay. But the boss still had a little reservation of Dick.

"He is new in the game that we are playing," said the truckers, "a dangerous and expensive game, and the boss wants to be sure."

I assumed that Will was using as his first name, Dick. Knowing the name he was using now was a considerable asset to my next plan of attack. I was going to watch the garage and try to find the location where they were keeping Will. Then I was going to have to devise a plan to bust him loose and not get either one of us killed. I checked the area where the garage was located and found a semi-run-down hotel, but good enough to house me during my surveillance time. It looked cheap, and the service was cheap. No bar or dining room, just a flophouse. I could see the garage out of the window of the hotel after I had washed it clean. I hoped people wouldn't notice how much cleaner my window was than the rest of the hotel's windows. So I sat behind the window, watching the trucks come and go, hoping to catch sight of Will in one of the trucks. It was a boring assignment that I had placed upon myself, but I had to start somewhere. After a few days sitting at the clean window, I saw a cattle truck pull up in front of the garage, and three men got out of the cab. One of the men was Will. I sat there and watched, and after about ten minutes, they came out the side door and went around and back of the garage. I thought to myself, *Maybe that's where the men are staying, and these two are perhaps Wills unknown guards since they wouldn't let him out on his own.* I might as well go on over to the garage and ask if they had any openings and get their replies. I was trying to figure a way to get Will away for a few minutes so I could tell him where I was staying, and even then I didn't know if they will let him out of their sight, so it might be difficult for him to reach me. I knew they had been out on cattle run but not necessarily a rustler run, but I could see fresh cattle manure on the side of the trucks rack and knew they had been somewhere recently, hauling cattle. Of course, there was nothing unusual about that, since it was a cattle hauling company. It was what they did on the side that mattered—perhaps hauling stolen cattle? We must have the hard proof of their thievery.

I must devise a method to talk to Will. I thought of a lot of different scenarios on how to get Will by himself. But after thinking them out, I didn't believe they would pan out. I had to think of something more devious than the rustlers. And of course, I was not a trained detective. I must try to use what common sense I was born with. I knew all things being equal, I could handle two or three men at the same time, so I was going to go over to the office, brazen my way through, asking for Dick, and saying, I didn't know what last name he was using at this time but I must talk to him for a few minutes. They were very. very suspicious about who I was, where I came from, what I was doing there, how I knew he was there, and what I wanted to speak to Dick about. I told them that these things were confidential, but it was urgent that Dick knew this information. Before they brought Will to the office, they requested that I took off my gun belt and place it on the manager's desk. To me, that was an unfriendly act and led me to believe that the outcome of this meeting was not going to be peaceful. I replied to the request, thinking all along about my knives inside my shirt collar and also on my belt, and no one knew about the knife in the pocket that I had the saddlemaker sew in my boot top, which was another throwing knife, so really I had three weapons at my disposal, if I got a chance to use them.

As Will came into the room, I got up quickly and said, "Dick, how are you doing?"

Will said, "Okay, Bill, what are you doing here?"

I said, "I have some information that's very important and confidential that I need to talk to you about. Dick, can we go somewhere and be alone?"

The truckers didn't seem to like that idea very much, and they said, "Talk here. If you have anything important to say, we would like to know what it is."

I said, "This is for Dick's ears only. Why can't Dick and I discuss this in private?"

"You got a problem with that?"

I said, "No, I have no problem with that, except I never saw a job were an employee could not talk to a friend discreetly."

The manager said, "This is a different circumstance. Dick is working on a confidential program that we must keep under wraps."

I said, "What is so confidential about a cattle hauling business that must be kept under wraps? I don't understand."

I could tell that the four men working for the cattle company were getting very edgy, and I looked at Will. He knew that this was festering into an all-out battle with the cattle company, and he was ready to do his part.

As we were talking, Will was easing his way toward the manager's desk, where he saw my gun belt was lying. Knowing him as well as I do, I knew he was going to try for my weapon, and he knew I was going to use my throwing knives, and he was thankful of that because he had been figuring that morning he might be in trouble. He had asked a lot of questions, which he thought had made the truck drivers suspicious of him, and with me showing up, that was the icing on the cake. I realized that this was long odds, especially with me being without my gun. It was four armed men against two unarmed men, and we would have to be very lucky if we come out of this unscathed. I tried to decide which cowboy I wanted to take out first, who looked more dangerous. I didn't want to kill the owner or manager of the cattle company, as I needed him for information. I hadn't planned this coming to a head as fast as it had, but I could not let Will be in jeopardy as I thought he was.

I decided, good or bad, that I would use my belt knife first. I could reach it quickly and get it on the way. While I reached for the knife behind my neck under my shirt, with these two knives flying in the air, landing approximately the same time, it would create a diversion, I thought, for Will to grab my gun off the manager's desk. I chose, after delivering my knives to their appropriate location, to dive across the desk toward the manager. I also had my knife that I carried in the top of my boot. I had a slit in the right side of my pant leg for easy access to the knife. As I sprang toward the manager, I pulled that knife, and in knocking the manager, to the floor, I pressed that knife to his throat. Will had reached my gun and shot the other cowboy's dead. We had three dead cowboys and a very scared manager in the room. I pulled my two knives out of the dead cowboy's bodies and wiped the blades clean on their shirts.

Will and I questioned the owner or manager, or whatever he was, of the cattle company as to the rustling of the cattle belonging to the railroad. The jig was up. We could no longer hide our identity, so we made it very clear that we wanted all the information that he possessed under threat, you might say, of bodily harm. With the killing of his three cohorts in crime, he knew or believed we were not going to beat around the bush. The answers must be forthcoming in detail—who was involved in the rustler's scheme. We looked through all of his papers; we found where he had made payments to the foreman of the ranch and the ranch manager also. Will and I contacted the authorities; the evidence was overwhelming. The opportunity for a large amount of cash at one time had turned their heads and made them criminals. Will and I went to the ranch, found Jack out on the range, and told him what had transpired and that we were going to contact the president of the railroad.

I sent the president of the railroad a telegram and told him, "Job accomplished, we feel you should partition the judge of this county to receive what funds may be left in the cattle company's bank account, as reimbursement for your rustling losses, but I'm sure you already thought of that."

He sent a telegram back, saying, "Sending my legal team to handle all details, your advice is well taken, please return to the home office so we can discuss our options." He signed the telegram, "Your friend and employer."

After returning to the home office, we were ushered into the president's office with great fanfare. He got up from his desk, walked around the desk shook, each of our hands, and said what a magnificent quick job you three have done—you have fulfilled my faith in you three. I'm going to release an article to the newspapers about your unerring devotion to your jobs, whatever they may be."

Bill said, "Yes, Mr. President, but we don't want any photographs taken of any of us in case we need to go undercover again, for you or for your associates. We can change our name, but it's difficult to change our looks."

So a news release was given to the papers in the greater area. It read,

Again, the three intrepid detectives of the modern West have struck again. They have exposed the very large rustling combine that has been stripping the Staked Planes of its cattle, and the rustlers have been using modern methods to enhance their success. The three detectives hired by the Old Minnesota railroad are William Chestnut, Jack Sundown, and their friend Will, and of course, their dog, Major. They dug out the facts and all that were involved. Unfortunately, they had to kill three of the rustlers in self-defense but managed to capture the man in charge, and he gave a list of the recipients, and they are now in jail awaiting trial. The president of the railroad, stockholders, and, indeed, all Westerners should be thankful for these untiring men. They are the same men who broke up a women slave trade ring in Portland, saved a train from being robbed by a gang of cutthroats, captured horse thieves, broke up another gang of rustlers, and have done many more civic duties. They are in our thoughts and prayers, there are not many men like this left anywhere in the West.

This newspaper column would be read throughout the Western United States. The three of us was given each a sizable bonus for our quick work on rounding up the rustlers.

We were told to take a few days off relax and come see the president of the railroad in one week for other assignments. I had found out what finishing school Patricia had been sent. I decided that I should write her a letter explaining what we had done in the past month or so.

I started out saying, "Patricia, my heart has been crying out for you loudly. Of course, I am the only one that can hear its mournful cry, but the noise it makes in my head is sometimes deafening. I don't know if your heart feels the same as mine, but I suspect it does. We are so much alike. The time we have been apart has been slow as a land tortoise's journey. I try to push the endearing thoughts of you out of my mind, for my own sanity, but to no avail. Our assignment for the railroad was to travel to the Staked Plains of Texas and catch a rustler's combine raking the cattle off the range with a modern method. With total cooperation with Will, Jack, and I we were able to catch the rustlers and all who were affiliated with them and put them in jail. We also managed to get some of the money that had been paid for the stolen cattle retrieved for the railroad. I don't know yet where our next assignment is going to be, but I'm going to tell the president of the railroad that if it is not somewhere in the vicinity of Boston, I'm going to resign my detective position and come wherever you are. My absence from you is unbearable. I have been saving my salary, my bonuses, my rewards, my bounties, and I have a sizeable nest egg, so we can get started together for the rest of our lives. I will accept nothing from your family, we will make it together as was destined. All my love, Bill."

The week that followed was a week that was uncertain for the three of us. I told Will and Jack my plans, that I was going to talk to the president of the railroad explained my feelings as best I could; and although I did not want to break up the three of us and our investigative team, it was imperative that I go to Boston if only for a few days. I hoped the president of the railroad would understand my feelings and that he had been in love in his younger years and hopefully still is.

We met with the president of the railroad. He again expressed his appreciation for a job well done. We told him that we were ready for a new assignment, and I especially told him that I would like the assignment to be by the way of Boston so I could go see Patricia; it's something that I must do. He said that he understood my feelings perfectly, and there was something in the Boston greater area that needed to be straightened out.

The Old Great Minnesota Railroad was in partners with a smaller railroad, the Boston-Maine railroad, but a profitable one and it was being sabotaged. He would like the three of us to go there and find out who was doing the dirty work. He told me that our time was our own, but he would like the problem solved quickly, as it was cutting deeply into their profits. He gave us a written report from the other railroad stating the kind of problems that they were having, which we read in its entirety. We told the president that we would need some instruction in the building of the railroad so we could act the part of the railroad gang. We could learn the art of railroad repair by studying with the Gandy dancers. If we could join a Gandy dancer gang of the Boston-Maine railroad, we might learn valuable information. He thought that was an excellent idea and said, "I will send a letter to the head of the Boston Maine railroad, instructing him to put you on not as a detective, because we still want to keep that under wraps."

So we packed up our gear in the boxcar along with our horses, and we chose a Pullman car with sleeping quarters for our trip to Boston. They had a wonderful dining car and a saloon car hooked to the train, of which we availed ourselves. We knew that the East was becoming very mechanical, like cars and such, but we preferred our horses; it was hard to give up something you know and love. We had our identification. We had our vouchers, and we had the letter to the president of the Boston-Maine railroad. We checked in to a local hotel. We were almost ready to start our investigations.

I had to find Patricia. Her finishing school was the Eastern University for Young Women. It was supposed to be a prestigious school catering to etiquette and fine arts. It was a coeducational school. I took a local conveyance to the school, walked into the lobby, and asked the young lady sitting at the desk if I could see Patricia O'Brien? She informed me that Patricia was in class at the present time, and I would have to return if I wanted to see her after class.

I told the young lady at the desk, "My name is Bill Chestnut, and I'm a friend of Patricia, and when could I please see her?"

Would she relay the message to Patricia, that I had been there and asked for her, and I said, I'd be back.

I went across the street from the school to a small restaurant and ordered something frivolous to eat, waiting for her class time to pass; it would be about an hour and a half. I was worried about her feelings for me since she had come East and met other young men that were more refined than me. I just wanted to be "cowboy." My feelings for her had not changed. I was wondering if Tom O'Brien had been correct. Does time and distance change everything?

Maybe I was jumping to conclusions; maybe I was not. I believed I was just scared of her reaction to me after our absence from each other. I was more scared of meeting her now than when I met the rustlers, horse thieves, and the train robbers who were trying to kill me and Will. I didn't know what to expect. But I must bite the bullet and face her, good or bad. I finished my toast and coffee, paid my bill, walked across the street, and sat down in the lobby waiting for Patricia. I saw her walking down the hall with another young man, and they were chatting merrily, or so it seemed to me. My heart did a double take, and it fell to its lowest level. I thought she had found someone to take my place. I guess I was jealous. She saw me and turned in my direction but did not run or walk faster toward me than she had been walking before. My common sense said something was wrong. She was not anxious to see me.

She said, "Bill, it's so nice to see you." She looked over at her companion and said, "This is a friend of mine, Bill Chestnut, who worked on my father's ranch in Eastern Oregon along with his first cousin, Bobby. Bill, this is Joe Edwards, a fellow student here at the University. We have several classes together."

I was dumbfounded at her nonchalant manner, and I replied, "Happy to meet you, Joe," although under my breath I had other evil thoughts.

Joe said, "Glad to meet you, Bill. I've have read in our newspapers about some of your exploits. It must be an exciting life out on the lonesome plains," as if he knew anything about the lonesome plains.

"Patricia here is a beautiful, wonderful, and intelligent, girl, and I like having her here at school immensely."

I said, "Yes, she is beautiful, and we think a lot of each other." I said, "Patricia, I have come to see you as I promised, I had the president of the railroad, James J. Hill route me to Boston especially so we could have some quality time together. Will, Jack, and I are assigned a new endeavor, which will take us perhaps a month to accomplish, and I couldn't stand the thought of not seeing you within that time period."

Patricia said, "Oh, Bill, that's wonderful. I'm sure you, Will, and Jack, will do a great job for the railroad. If you have the chance, please come back and see me after your mission has been accomplished, as I know it will."

I said to myself, *Is this all the enthusiasm that I get?*

I was so upset I couldn't think straight I couldn't and didn't think of anything to say at this particular time. I thought to myself, *What a horrible thing, our relationship is over, what a terrible tragedy.*

I was truly devastated.

I said to Joe Edwards, "Treat her with dignity, or you will answer to me. If you look up my record, you'll find twenty-three dead men that I have put down, don't make it twenty-four. I'm sure you get my meaning. Goodbye, Patricia."

I tipped my hat, turned on my heel, and walked away with a broken heart. She didn't even call out goodbye. The trail that I would travel now would only be chosen by me, Will, and Jack. I was on my own.

Upon returning to the hotel where Will and Jack and I were staying, I went to our room; no one was there. I sat in the chair and put my head in my hands down on the table top and felt unbelievable despair. All my dreams of a long life with Patricia was gone. Will and Jack found me that way, and I blurted out the happenings, and I sat there for a couple of hours, thinking of my actions or inactions. What went wrong? The boys were very sympathetic because both knew my feelings for Patricia.

They said, "We'll see you at six o'clock in the dining room. We're sorry."

What went wrong and what direction this had gone, I didn't know. I vowed that I couldn't let my feelings get in the way of Jack's and Will's employment and prospects, and again I would have to bite the bullet and go forward. At fifteen minutes to six, I got up from the chair, straightened up my clothes, washed my face dried my eyes, and went to the dining room to meet the boys. I myself was no longer a boy. I was a man, and I must act like one, no matter the adversities and the wretched feelings.

The next morning, the three of us went to the office of the Boston-Maine railroad president. We showed him our credentials and the letter from James J. Hill, who was his superior in the pecking order. We told him our assignments and our thoughts and told him according to the letter he was to hire us as new Gandy dancers. No one—and we meant, no one—other than he should know our true identity. We wanted to learn the railroad trade as Gandy dancers and perhaps locate some of the Boston-Maine railroad problems. Secrecy was a matter of life or death. He told his secretary to call his top foreman and have him in his office in about an hour.

Upon arriving, the president introduced the three of us, saying, "Put these three gentlemen on as Gandy dancers wherever you think the need arises, teach them the business from the ground up."

"Yes, sir, come with me men, the lessons start now," said the foreman.

He took us to the bunkhouse and introduced us to the balance of the crew. Now was where we must be careful. It was a salty-looking crew. The head man was a large Irishman, not long from the emerald island, with a large red nose depicting he liked his booze but had learned his business well. He was a gruff, no-nonsense boss, and that was what you called him: "boss."

He assigned us our tools, shovels, picks, tongs, spikes, and some other items, and said, "Keep them clean and sharp, they are the tools of your trade."

"And believe me, they could also be tools of murder," said Jack.

The Gandy tool was a steel rod about five feet long with a crossbar across the bottom, using the tool required placing a foot on the bar and hopping around the roadbed like a pogo stick, hence "gaudy dancing," realigning of the railroad rails from excessive use.

We kept our horses and our pack mule in the livery stable of the railroad. They would be well cared for. Major would keep in the bunkhouse with us, and we had no objections from the members of the crew. He was more like a mascot. We were informed the night before that we would be going to be assigned a section of track to inspect and repair as necessary, and we would be gone around five to seven days.

"Pack up your personal gear that you need and your tools of the trade, we will be leaving early the next morning."

We had discussed before, that we would not seem to know each other, that we were individuals that had been hired by the president of the Boston-Maine. We did not want to give our positions away, nor the fact that we had been friends, until necessary—then believe me, they would know we were friends.

I decided that now would be a good time to write Bobby a letter back at the Double O Bar Ranch.

Dear Bobby,

Many things have happened since we last saw each other. Hope you have recovered completely from your ordeal at the Pendleton Roundup Rodeo. As you may know, Jack and Will are with me. We are now working for the Old Great Minnesota Railroad, president, James J. Hill. We are working undercover on some projects that he wants us to handle. Most of them are dangerous projects, and I'm so happy to have Will and Jack with me. We have finished a project on the Staked Plains in Texas. We have rounded up a cattle-rustling cartel where they were using cattle trucks as a means of transporting the cattle from the range to the slaughterhouses. We have accomplished that and given a full report to the railroad. The railroad released a newspaper article on the three of us and our accomplishments. I don't know if it was reprinted in your newspaper or not. We have been assigned to a job in Boston, Massachusetts. On my insistence, we were assigned the job of looking into the sabotage happenings on the Boston-Maine railroad, which is a subsidiary of the Old Great Northern. This gave me a chance to go by the finishing school where Patricia is attending classes. I did that and talked to her briefly. She was with a young man who is also a student at the school, and she seemed to be taken with him. I was introduced to this young man whose name is Joe Edwards. Patricia was cool toward me, not like when we worked at the ranch. I told her that I had made a special trip with the permission of the railroad president to see her as I promised I would. She seemed to have little interest in my endeavors, and I bid her goodbye. Maybe Tom O'Brien was right, it was a devastating moment in my life. I guess I'm just not interesting enough for her.

We three are learning to be Gandy dancers, working on the railroad bed that was in need of repair. We were hoping in that way, we could get a line on the individuals who were doing the sabotage incidents. It had to be a very secretive operation, or we could run into serious trouble. We were being treated very well by the railroad.

Actually, from one job to the other, we're living in the lap of luxury and were being paid well and left to our own devices in rooting out the criminals. We were saving our money; the railroad was paying most of our expenses. I'm sorry, Bobby, that I disrupted your life on the ranch, and it seems like every life that I touched. That was not my intention when I started out to renew our relationship and friendship. My feelings toward you have not diminished in any fashion, and someday, I look forward to seeing you again. I just wanted you to know where I am, where Will and Jack are, and the outcome with my meeting with Patricia. My feelings for her have not changed, but I fear the rift between us is wide and may never be closed. I remain your cousin and friend, Bill C.

I awoke the next morning with trepidation in my subconscious mind. Today was the first day of our learning experience as Gandy dancers. I had very little idea as to what we were going to be called upon to do when starting our learning experience. I could tell from the manner of the boss that it was not going to be a picnic; we had a job to do, and the boss was going to see that it is completed to the best of his ability. The safety of the passengers and crew was in our hands. It could be a very small thing left undone that could cause a terrific tragedy. The Gandy dancers only worked four months out of the year, and their pay was an average of $44 a month, which was just a little better than the pay of a cowboy of a dollar a day and found. A cowboy worked all year, and the Gandy dancers only four months out of the year. The railroad always kept several crews the year round, and each worker hoped he would be chosen as a full-time employee They were out of work until the next season, and they take what extra jobs they could find in the meantime. It was tough on them and their families to make a living. They were ethnic groups such as Chinese, Irish, African Americans, Mexicans, and Native Indians—all worked on a Gandy Dancer crew. I could see and understand why some of the crew might turn to the shady side of the fence if additional pay was involved. It was part of the foreman and crew boss to see that didn't happen. However, there were too many opportunities. They couldn't catch all the "unintentional mistakes" as they called them. The dancers worked at the scene with the chant of the lead singer.

They were songs that came from Africa, Ireland, and other ethnic songs as the dancers were working their Gandy tool. Straightening the rails, they would place the tip of the rod under the rail, and at the chant of the singer in a rhythmic manner, all would push their Gandy tools at the same time, to move the rail a minute distance. They would do this over and over on the same rail until it was back in its original position and spike it down. Then they would go to the next rail and do it all over again. These chanters or singers had such a large repertoire they would go all day and not give the same chant twice. It was believed that the African Americans on the Gandy dancers crews started the blues, telling about all their hardships on the rails and their lives, in musical rhythm.

Believe me, the next day after working with the Gandy rod, my muscles were sore, and I found some new muscles I didn't even know I had. It was hard work, and it took me several days to get rid of the soreness. Will, Jack, and I were cordial to each other, but we were not overly friendly by design. We didn't want to give ourselves away to our crew or other crews that were in the vicinity. The crew boss was fair. He didn't give us any harder jobs than he gave other members of the crew. Jack, being a Native American, became friendly with some other Native Americans on a neighboring crew. He spent as much time as he thought necessary to gather any pertinent information as to why the line was being sabotaged. He acted as if he was down and out financially and would be open to make some additional money, and as much as we were going to be employed by the railroad four months out of the year, he would need more money for the rest of the year. A lot of the Gandy dancers found other jobs in the meantime and did not return to work for the railroad. He told us in private, Will and I, that he believed he was making some progress. Jack said that some of the Native Americans had more money than the railroad was paying; they could buy some of the finer things of life that most workers couldn't afford. It didn't look or speak well for a few of the Native American employees, but most of them were honest. There were bad apples in most bushels. Jack disliked the fact that there was dishonesty in the Native Americans, since he held most of them in high esteem for their honesty. We suggested to Jack that he follow through on this course of action and see where it led. If and when he needs either of us, we would make ourselves available.

Several weeks had passed. Will and I had kept our ears to the ground, listening to members of our crew and members of any other crew that we came in contact with, but could find no fresh signs of complicity. As of now, Jack's Native Americans were the only leads that we had. One evening after chow, sitting around the bonfire that we had built along the tracks, we had our crew boss to ourselves. We asked him about the sabotage that had been going on with this railroad. We had heard about it before we were hired on, and we had heard some things after we were hired.

He said, "It is a strange thing that so many accidents plague this line."

We asked him, "Why do you think this is happening?"

He said, "I don't think it's the luck of the Irish. I think perhaps it's had some help."

We asked, "What do you mean by that?"

He said, "I have worked on other railroads as a Gandy dancer, and this railroad has far too many accidents for it to be a natural occurrence."

I said, "What is your given name boss, all we know is boss, and you are that."

He said, "My name is from the old sod. It's Mick Murphy. What good does that do you?"

I said, "Mick we three have been debating on telling you something of grave importance, this is something that you need to swear on the faith of your Emerald Island that you won't tell anyone."

"If this is that important, I will swear with my word and heart," said Mick. Mick.

"My name is Bill Chestnut, this is Jack Sundown, and this is one of our very good friends, his name is Will. We are personal railroad detectives of the Old Great Northern Railroad under orders of James J. Hill, president of the railroad and also the owner of Boston-Maine Railroad. We are his personal detectives sent here to find out why this branch of the railroad has had so many "accidents". This information we're giving you now could be our death warrants. But in our observation of you, the time we have been here on this crew, you have gained our respect and trust. That is why we wanted your solemn pledge not to divulge this information to anyone. We have shown our identification papers to the head of the Boston-Maine railroad only, and we have sworn him to the same silence that we have sworn you. Not even the foreman knows our true identity. Our purpose here is to find who is behind these sabotage acts, from the bottom thoughout the top echelon, wherever the fault lies. We three have the authority to take over the running of this entire Boston-Maine railroad if the need arises. We don't believe it will come to that. But be prepared if it does. We would like to hear from you any and all matters no matter how small or unimportant you may think it is, tell us of any improprieties that you have seen or heard or thought. We reiterate, no member of your crew or anyone else must know our true identity, is that understood?"

"Yes, it is," said Mick, "you can trust me."

"You continue treating us as one of your crew, is that understood?" I said.

"Yes, I will," said Mick, "but that will be hard to do, knowing now what I do."

"That's great," I said. "Ask everyone on the crew if they have seen anything out of the ordinary as far as actions or actual incidents, any clue may be of extreme importance. You know, Mick, that any questions may arouse suspicion and put you in danger, so be very careful how you question the crew, one of them may be a traitor. Jack, you continue to talk to the Native Americans and let them know that you are a good friend of War Chief Sitting Bull and that you just left him a few months ago for him to work for the Buffalo Bill Wild West Show. That way they will believe that you are no friend of the white man and may open up and give you some pertinent valuable information. Will and I did some checking around, trying to find who has most to gain by these sabotaging acts. We must continue to do our job on the Gandy dancers crew, we cannot afford to arouse suspicion. The Native Indians in the other crew speak a little English, but they also know hand sign. They are Cherokee, and you are Lakota Sioux, but I'm sure you can understand each other's hand signs. You know how to get in their good graces."

Will and I left Jack to his own designs, we knew he would do a good job. Given the opportunity, there was a lesser commuter train who had just started hauling some freight, and they were cutting into the passenger and freight from the Boston-Maine railroad. We decided on our own time to ride their rails and ask any information that we could about the desirability of the Boston-Maine railroad. Will and I continued asking questions about the route, how the passengers liked the facilities and numerous other questions, hoping to get a line on what was happening to the Boston-Maine railroad.

Most of the passengers on the local commuter stated they were afraid of the accidents that had been happening on the Boston-Marine, and the freight companies said they were tired of losing cargo. We concluded that the commuter railroad definitely had a hand in the sabotage. It was now time to prove it.

Jack Sundance had been working his way into the confidence of the Native Americans during this time, and they had told him that they would introduce him to the superintendent of the commuter line, and if he wanted to make a deal, the superintendent would be the one to speak to. Jack learned from the other Indians that the superintendent on the commuter railroad was paying a sum of $120, which would tie the Indians over until the next Gandy dancer crew that went to work in the spring. This information was invaluable, and the three of us decided that our next conversation would be with superintendent of the commuter line, which wasn't long in coming. We confided our information to Mick Murphy, our Gandy dancer boss, so if something happened to us along the way, he could forward this information to James J. Hill, president of the Old Great Minnesota Railroad. He said he would do that, but he didn't think it would be necessary.

The three of us took turns in following the superintendent of the commuter railroad. We knew his daily routine as well as we knew our own. We described our purpose in snatching him in an advantageous location to us—I meant, we picked him up without a fight. I told him we wanted to be in an area where his screams wouldn't be heard and we would not be interrupted with our painful questioning of him.

"Painful for you, not us, if you don't do as you're told."

I told Will that if you let your captive knew what was coming at the beginning of the interrogation, you had an easier task at the end. I told the superintendent that Jack Sundance was an uncivilized Lakota Sioux straight from War Chief Sitting Bull's reservation, and he was going to do the questioning in the Sioux custom fashion—that Will and I were going to go outside so we couldn't hear the screams and stand guard. By the time that we had undressed him, at least down to his waist, he became very talkative. The Easterners still believed the stories that they had read in the newspapers about the Indian torture methods. In other words, he spilled the beans.

He told us what we wanted to know, who was involved, their names, and implicated management in the commuter line, to the highest level. We had him sign a confession naming all the personnel that was involved in the sabotage events. We would use the confession against all the criminals at their trials. (We didn't have to lay a finger on him during interrogation; he did not look forward to Jack's Sioux method of questioning.) Funny what the mind would conjure up especially if you're guilty. We took the prisoner back to our Gandy dancer camp and told Mick what we had learned, let him read the signed confession, and told him we were taking the superintendent to the president of the Boston-Maine railroad and asked him if he would like to come along.

He said, "Yes, I would be honored to go, along with a couple of my men, just to be sure the superintendent does not escape. Not that I doubt your ability."

We said, "Sure bring them along, the more the merrier."

The president of the Boston-Maine railroad was astonished with our headway and the arrest and confession of the superintendent of the commuter line. He immediately called the police department, and they sent a lieutenant and two police officers over to pick the prisoner up and go arrest the additional people that was named in the confession. They had everything they needed for a conviction. It was going to be a murder charge in as much as some people had lost their lives in the sabotage incidents. I told the president of the Boston-Maine railroad to send a telegram to James J. Hill of the Great Northern Railroad saying, "Assignment accomplished. You may be able to buy commuter line at a good price. I'm not a businessman like you, but maybe a golden opportunity to increase revenue. Signed Bill, Will, Jack. Waiting next assignment, reach us here in Boston.

I said, "Boys, if we lose our jobs as railroad detectives, we can always get a job as a Gandy dancer."

They laughed and said, "We don't much like your humor, Bill."

The police reporter, after the roundup of all the criminals working for the commuter line, wrote an article about the three of us breaking the sabotage ring. He did a little background check and also included some of our other exploits, which I guessed might be some entertainment for his readers.

The next day we received a telegram from Mr. Hill, stating, "Job well done, taking your advice, sending legal team in regard to commuter line. Take some rest, will be contacting you soon. Your friend, Jim."

We told the president of the B-M railroad of our discussion with Mick Murphy. We suggested that the railroad raise his salary to $60 a month and keep him on their payroll the year round, that we considered him to be a truthful, honorable man and would be an asset to the railroad. The president said that would be done. Mick was very grateful for his newly earned status.

I had been thinking about Patricia and if I should make an additional attempt to talk to her. I had been very heartbroken by her attention to me the last time we had met. After the three of us had settled into our hotel room for a little rest and recuperation, I would contact her again as my feelings for her had not diminished during my Gandy dancing days. I told Will and Jack that I was going to the university to see if I could speak to her and get the true story, not allowing my heart to be on my sleeve exposed.

So now I was at the university going up to the front desk to ask if I could see Patricia O'Brien. I asked the girl at the desk if I could see Patricia. She looked at me in an astonished fashion.

She said, "Haven't you heard?"

I said, "Heard what?"

She said, "Patricia is in Saint Mary's Hospital after she had a molestation attack by four men."

I was shocked beyond words. I stumbled out of the university hallway to the street. I sat on a campus bench, trying to understand what I had just heard. It was like a searing branding iron going through my head over and over, my Patricia. At least I'd considered her mine for many many months, the minute after we had first met. Her being subjected to that horror was beyond comprehension. I lost all track of time. It was getting late in the afternoon, and I knew I had to go back to the hotel and tell Will and Jack this horrific news. I decided to go by the Boston Tribune newspaper and get all that was written about this attack. Having done that without identifying myself, I tucked the newspaper under my arm and went back to the hotel. I had plans to make. There was going to be hell unleashed in Boston, Massachusetts. When I got to my room, the boys were gone, which gave me the opportunity I needed to read the article from the newspaper over and over again, not to miss a word or name.

Joe Edwards, a student at the university, and three of his friends—the only other name she knew was Ron—were the perpetrators to this terrible act. The police have an all-points bulletin out for their arrest, but I, Bill Chestnut, would have an unsympathetic hand in their final retribution.

I left the hotel room and went to find Mick Murphy.

He was in the barracks owned by B-M railroad, and I took him aside and said, "Mick, I'm going to ask you a favor. You don't have to do this if you don't want, but I need your help."

He said, "Bucko, whatever you need, I'm here to help."

I showed him the newspaper, which he read to his consternation.

He said, "Bill, this is beyond words. What do you want me to do?"

I said, "Mick I want to find these four men desperately. I would like you to get your Gandy dancers, even other than your own crew, to search this city from top to bottom to find these attempted murderers and rapists. I will place a reward of $500 on Joe Edwards's head, alive, and $200 on the heads of each participant, alive. I mean to find these bastards. Mick, this is very important to me. I know you understand my meaning, being a devout Irishman."

"Yes, Bill," said Mick, "you can count on me and my men not to leave any stones unturned until we find them."

"That's great, Mick, I don't want you or your men to arrest them, it might be dangerous, just inform me as to their location. I'll do the rest."

The die was cast, Gandy dancers would be spreading out over the entire city with unwavering determination to find these bastards. I had gotten a recent university photograph of Joe Edwards, had copies made, and distributed them to my Gandy dancers. They would find him; I had no doubt.

Will and Jack back at the hotel room were waiting for me. They were incensed, they had read a copy of the newspaper I left in the room. They extend their sympathy and their help in rounding up the perpetrators.

I told them, "No, I accept your condolences in the way that I know you gave it." I said, "I don't want you to get involved in what I might do, even knowing that you would be ready and willing to help me any way you can. This is my responsibility, I must handle it myself. I don't know yet what my heart and brain will let me do under these circumstances. You may not see me for a few days, but don't be worried, you are my two best, most trustworthy friends who may also be interrogated as to my whereabouts and what you know about me. Just say to those who ask (ask me no questions and I'll tell you no lies), we know nothing. You may have to put up with a little harassment from the authorities, but I trust you completely. I'm going to have to find another room to live in for the time being. I can't come back to this hotel. They'll have it watched. I can't do what I must if I'm being watched by the authorities."

I gathered up my immediate personal gear, had Will and Jack be a lookout for me as I slipped down the back entrance of the hotel, and started walking several blocks before I caught a carriage to another hotel, a little closer to the other side of the tracks. Of course, Major was with me. After checking into the room, I contacted Mick and told him my new hotel room addresses and if he had any information, he could contact me there. Sitting there alone in the sparsely furnished hotel room, I began feeling despondent, thinking about all that could have been, what could never be, what was now out of my grasp, because of the indecent desires of these four despicable inhuman beings. I was thinking of what punishment they should have for this deed. I thought of killing all four, and then I thought, *No, that's too easy, they wouldn't have to live with what they had done, they should have to spend the rest of their lives making atonements.* Did they really know the cost of their actions, or care? Was it only their own warped lust that they were thinking about? The more I thought of the punishment, the madder I got. It was like something that was eating at my soul, and I had to put a stop to it. Could I be the judge and jury? My demented mind said yes.

I'd stayed in this rat-infested room—if you could call it that— for the last three days with no word from Mick. I couldn't eat or sleep in this state of mind. I was ready to go out and look for Edwards myself, come hell or high water. I didn't believe the authorities were looking for me yet, but I wanted to keep myself incommunicado if at all possible. There would be a time when I will be on their wanted list. I saw a folded paper being slipped underneath my door, and I cautiously went to the door and picked it up. I unfolded the paper, and it read, "Found our trash, meet me at the Shamrock saloon." My heart was pounding, and my hands were shaking. I was sure the lack of food has something to do with my physical condition, but my brain was working time and a half.

I walked to the saloon and saw Mick sitting at a table at the far end of the room. He had a beer that he was nursing, and he waved me to sit down.

Mick said, "Bucko, we have found our query. I have three men guarding his location, but he has not been apprehended as you requested."

"Perfect," I said. "I knew I could trust you and your men."

Mick said, "Bill, can I buy you a drink?"

I said, "Mick, normally, I don't drink, but on this occasion out of our friendship, I'll have a small shot of whiskey. I may need its fortification for later." I held the dram of whiskey up and said, "Salute, Mick, may you be in the arms of God before the devil knows you're dead. Here's your $500, I'll leave it up to you how to distribute it to your men. Mick, where can I get a writing tablet and a pencil, I'm going to have this bastard write a full confession on what he has done and name the other three participants. I'm going to turn him and his confession over to the authorities after I have finished my retribution."

I acquired the necessary stationery and all that was left was to confront Joe Edwards. I decided that I would wait for the early hours of the morning before accosting him. I told Mick to keep his men posted around the house so Edwards could not escape, and I would deal with him in the early hours of the morning.

The time had come for Joe Edwards and me to meet for the second time. It was about two thirty in the morning. There was no moon. It was dark, very dark. I went by Mick's guards and slipped in the back door quietly. It was like walking into the pits of hell. I struck a country match to get the lay of the room, and what I saw disgusted me. Lying on the bed was Joe Edwards in a pile of filthy bedclothes, and you could tell that he had been drinking heavy. You could tell a drunken snore if you had ever heard one before. Strewn about the floor were whiskey bottles—empty, of course; partially eaten food, newspapers, clothes, junk, and of course, his houseguests, which were two large rats scampering about on the floor. I lit the only coal oil lamp in the room and turned the wick down low, so it wouldn't give off too much light at this moment. From the Double O Bar Ranch, I had brought along a pigging string made out of rawhide, which was used to tie up a calf on the range when you get ready to brand or castrate the calf to make a steer out of him, and I thought to myself how fitting it was a piece of rawhide from Patricia's father's ranch to tie him up snugly. I threw the crap off of the chair, which was the only one in the room, and sat down to wait. I wanted Joe Edwards to have a clear head for his retribution.

I sat there in the semidarkness with the notebook and pencil in my hand, and I started writing.

I said,

To whom it may concern:

After an extensive search on my part alone, I have found this cowardly inhuman being cowering here in this rat-infested hole that these Eastern cities allow. He and his three friends have done the inexplicable act of all time, he has taken the trust of a young, inexperienced girl and turned her over to his own lust and the lusts of his three cohorts, and after they had finished with her, they then tried to murder her so she couldn't tell of the dastardly deed or identify them. It is my duty as a citizen of this great nation and upholding the Constitution that the nation was built upon, to make a citizen's arrest and to give the punishment that he so sorely deserve. They have ruined this young girl's life. This action that I take today is my idea alone and has not been discussed with anyone. I do this in anger and for the protection of many young girls who may follow, keeping them out of these sex predators' hands is my goal. All men who value the decent lives of their sisters and daughters will hear my cry and let it be known to the world that we will not tolerate this kind of action again. If the other three predators, after reading this article in the *Boston Tribune*, do not turn themselves into the authorities with a signed confession, they will be subject to the same treatment their leader has suffered. You had better pray with all of your twisted heart that you never hear my name again. If you do, I promise you'll regret it. The Dark Avenger.

PS, I hope that the editor of the *Boston Tribune* has the cojones to print this message for the world to see. If not, I hope another newspaper will pick up this article and print it for all the decent women to read and take hope.

The piece of human filth was finally coming out of his drunken stupor. He was trying to move his arms and his legs and was finding that he had no power over them. They were tied by the wet rawhide, which was now drying out and shrinking into an ironlike chain. While he was in his stupor, I'd had used my sharpest knife to remove his trousers and undergarments, I keep my knives as sharp as a surgeons scalpel, I hone them at a 20 degree angle. He was now lying there exposed for the entire world to see. I had reluctantly donned my mask made out of his filthy pillowcase and placed it over my head. I knew he would know who I was, but he could not tell the authorities that he saw who his avenger was.

He woke up, mumbling, "Who are you? What's going on? What is this? What's happening? Who are you? What are you doing here?"

I said, "I am the Dark Avenger and your worst nightmare. If you follow my orders explicitly, you may live to tell of this meeting. If you don't follow my orders, you will be in excruciating pain for many hours before I finally kill your worthless life. I have a paper and pencil here at your disposal for you to write your tawdry confession. I want the names and addresses of all participants, and I'm going to turn your confession, and you, over to the authorities if you cooperate. If you do not cooperate, I will call the authorities to bring the coroner and undertaker to take what's left of your bloody body away to bury in a pauper's grave, even your family will not want your corpse after I have finished with it. Start writing."

And he did. Of course, in his confession, he tried to smooth things to his benefit, but everyone knew that he was a liar and worse. He gave the names of the other three participants and their addresses. He wrote his pathetic apologies using the age-old excuse that he was drunk and out of his senses. But that excuse didn't hold water; there were to many holes. I let him write for ten to fifteen minutes. I didn't want to deprive him of his right to speak in his own behalf. I could tell when his writing was getting almost illegible, and he was sweating like someone had poured water over his head. I didn't want to get the paper wet with his perspiration.

I took the paper and pencil away from Joe and said, "It's time to pay the piper, Joe."

He was whiter than the sheet he lay on.

I said, "Joe, being an educated university student like you are, you probably know what a eunuch is, so I don't have to explain. That's what you will be in a few minutes, I'm going to remove your testicles so you can never harm another young lady again."

I think you could hear his wail and cry all the way up the block. I quickly picked up one of his dirty socks and stuffed it into his mouth.

I said, "Joe, you're going to be a real treat for some of the inmates at the state prison when you get there. I think your name will be changed to Mary Jane, and they'll treat you with 'dignity,' as you did Patricia."

When he felt the cold razor sharp steel blade of my knife on his scrotum, he passed out, which was a good thing for him and me; it made things easier. It was getting daylight, and I looked out the window, and I saw an emaciated, hungry hound in the alley. With my gloved hand, I picked up Joe's testicles and threw them to the dog, and he ate them hungrily. I heated up one of the kitchen knives until it was red hot, and I cauterized the wounds so he wouldn't bleed to death before the police and medical help could arrive.

I then called on Mick to have one of his men deliver the letters to the chief of police. If asked, he would say, some man who he could not describe gave him the letter and $.50 for the delivery; that was all he knew. I had also given a duplicate confession and my article to another of Mick's men to deliver to the *Boston Tribune* editor, with the same story.

I then went back to my hole in the wall room south of the railroad tracks to await further developments, which I knew would come with a loud bang! The newspaper hawkers on the street corners, the next morning, were yelling their lungs out.

"Rapist found mutilated, read all the details, buy a paper."

It went on and on like that. The papers were flying out of the newsboys' hands. It was scandalous news. Boston's higher society could not read enough of the lurid details. Some thought it was barbaric; many more knew it was justified. I learned later that none of Mick's men had gotten into trouble; their tale was accepted as the truth. I contacted Mick again and gave him the other $600 for the location of the other three men, although his men didn't have too much to do with their capture. After they had read the article in the Boston Tribune and hearing by word of mouth what happened to Joe, their leader, they chickened out and gave themselves up with a written confession as I had demanded. There was no question in the minds of all Bostonians that these four men were guilty of the crime. Now the time was spent waiting for Joe Edwards to heal. If he was a steer on the ranch, he would heal completely in about a week; with a human anatomy, I had no idea. I learned by reading the local papers that Patricia was recovering and would be out of Saint Mary's Hospital sometime soon.

Her mother and father, along with their ranch foreman, Bobby Chestnut, had come to town to be with her during her recuperation. I personally didn't want to see Patricia. My heart was broken, and if I ever saw Thomas O'Brien again, I would probably kill him for what he unduly had caused. All this was his cause and effect. I decided to try and see Bobby. I knew that he knew where Will and Jack were staying. I had not seen or heard any more about me from the authorities. I decided to take a chance and contact Will and Jack. I decided to use a disguise as a Bostonian on the skids and slip into the hotel lobby and wait for either Will or Jack to make an appearance. I didn't believe I had to put on a lot of disguise because by this time, I was getting a little smelly and cruddy and looked very much down on my luck. I was getting the eye from the desk clerk and a few of the bellboys. They didn't like my looks dirtying up their clean lobby. Luckily, both Will and Jack came down the stairs at the same time, and I made an obvious move, which I knew Will would pick up on.

He strolled over to my vicinity and nonchalantly stood for second and said quietly, "Meet us across the street at the saloon."

I nodded my head as they left and went out the front door. I sat there for maybe five to ten minutes, and then I left and walked across the street to the saloon.

Will and Jack both were glad to see me and gave me a manly hug and said, "My god, Bill, where have you been, and what have you done?"

I said, "If you would buy me something to eat and a cup of coffee, I'd be happy to tell you something, but I just can't seem to get any service around here, even with my friends," and they both laughed.

They took me down the street to a restaurant, which I wouldn't really call a greasy spoon. It was probably a little better than that, but the food was delicious, anyway. I hadn't eaten anything in about a week. I stopped counting some days ago. I told them my story, leaving no details out. I told them about Joe Edwards, getting a signed confession from him, castrating him, feeding his testicles to the starving mutt.

"Hibernating for about three days trying to get myself together so I was ready to meet you two, you two are very important in my life."

I told them about reading the newspaper that Tom O'Brien and his wife were coming to Boston and that Bobby would be with them. I told them that I secretly told myself that if I saw Thomas O'Brien again, I was going to kill him. I told them I had read that Patricia was recuperating and that she would be ready about the same time that Joe Edwards was recuperating. I told them I was going to try and stay away from the trial and seeing no one except you two and Bobby, if that can be arranged.

I asked them if they had heard from James J. Hill of the railroad, and they said yes.

Will said, "He is 110 percent in your corner, Bill. He will do anything within his sizable power to get you and us out of this fix. He would like for us to report to his office in his railroad car on the side track in Tulsa, Oklahoma, as soon as we can make it. He has a large and profitable association in mind, and he wants to start it with us. He wouldn't tell us what his plans were until all three of us were together to discuss it. He understands that the three of us are bonded together solidly. It does sound intriguing."

I told Will and Jack that I would be moving back into this hotel with them as soon as possible. If the authorities want to question me, whom they undoubtedly will, I'd have to bite the bullet and tell them nothing. I was out of town on a job for the railroad.

"Do you think Mr. Hill will confirm that?"

Will and Jack both shook their heads, "Yes, undoubtedly."

After I cleaned up, I told Will and Jack that I was going to see the lieutenant in charge of this district in the police department. I didn't want to be any kind of a fugitive while working with them and for the railroad. I was bombarded with questions but gave little answers.

They said, "We have no evidence to hold you on or any charges, you may go," which was music to my ears and would give Will, Joe, and me the liberty we needed to continue our job with the Old Great Northern Minnesota Railroad and meeting Mr. Hill in Tulsa, Oklahoma.

Before I left Boston, I must talk to Bobby. I must explain to him what I have done and my feelings. I didn't want Bobby to have a false impression of my actions. Jack located Bobby's hotel room and asked Bobby if he would like to see me before the three of us left for Tulsa, Oklahoma.

"Yes, very much so," said, Bobby. "Where shall we meet?"

I said, "The hotel dining room will be fine. We may be interrupted by the police authorities, but everything will work out, so we set a date for tomorrow about five thirty in the evening."

I spent the next day refurbishing myself as I was a little rundown and lost a lot of weight, and I went to the local haberdashery and bought some clothes that would fit. I was ready to see Bobby when he walked into the dining room. We did our typical manly hug and said some niceties—which I confess I don't remember, nor what I heard because, I guess, I was in a fog, trying to bring my life together. Since leaving the farm at about sixteen years of age, plus or minus, up to now had been a whirlwind life experience, and I was only twenty-one years old. Bobby made the comment that he thought I was a little thinner than I should be, but we let it drop at that.

I said, "Bobby, a lot has happened since I wrote the last letter. Will, Jack, and I solved the sabotage ring on the Boston-Maine railroad. We brought them all to justice. When I returned to Boston, I got the horrific news about Patricia's ordeal, and it tore me apart. I haven't spoken to her, but I'm sure she knows I'm back in Boston. She knows, without me telling her, that I have avenged the atrocities that she had to endure. I did it the only way I knew how. I did it my way. Some people think I was too harsh, and some people don't. I leave it to everyone's own conscience, mine is clear. I don't want to see Patricia or her father, whom I have vowed in my own mind to kill for his colossal inhuman blunders. He and only he caused all this to happen in an indirect fashion. I don't think the authorities are going to arrest me or pin any of this fiasco on me, they have no hard evidence. With Will and Jack's okay, we're leaving Boston tomorrow for Tulsa, Oklahoma, where are meeting with Mr. Hill the president of the railroad. He states that he has a very ambitious program that he wants to lay out before us. He hasn't told us the details yet because he wants all three to be present, he knows we work as one. But I did want to meet with you, Bobby, try to explain myself, and look forward to writing you and meeting you again someday in the future."

"Yes," said Bobby, "as always, best of luck."

The next day, we booked passage on a train heading for Tulsa. We had gotten our horses and gear in a separate boxcar with a Pullman attached. We had instructed the conductor to let us off at Broken Arrow, Oklahoma. We wanted to ride our horses into Tulsa, and of course, Major hadn't had a good leg stretching run for some time. He was putting on weight from lack of exercise. And I'm ready for a new assignment to get my mind on other things. As usual, when you're riding by train, time travels slowly, but you do get to see the countryside and all of its good and bad. We speculated on what Mr. Hill had in mind for us to do this time. It had always been an exciting assignment that he had for us. But this assignment, unbeknownst to us, would change our lives greatly and forever.

The conductor came to our Pullman and said, "Broken Arrow is thirty minutes ahead, prepare for departure."

We were anxious to get back on the trail as range detectives and Gandy dancers and a host of other professions, but we always loved the cowboy's life; it got deep into your pores, and you fed on it for nourishment.

We off-loaded the horses and our gear and went into the town to find lodging. We found a hotel that had a saloon and a decent restaurant, and we paid for two nights. We thought we would get the feel of the range in this part of Oklahoma and catch up on the current news. The hotel also had a livery where we stabled our horses. We did have to pay two bits more a night to accommodate Major. After eating at the in-house restaurant, we strolled into the saloon.

We were surprised that most of the talk in the saloon was regarding the oil boom that was hitting the country. They were talking about oil, gas leases, buying land, wildcatting, and really, things we were not familiar with. It was time to learn. It was always my method of operation to keep the sheriff informed as to whom we were and what we were there for. We each had our customary drink and listened to the customers in the saloon. Some were dressed as cowboys, but most, I guess, were dressed as oilmen. They were talking about large amounts of money to be made overnight. In riding to the hotel, we had passed the sheriff's office; and after our drinks, we decided we should pay the sheriff a visit. I always thought it better if you go to the sheriff than have the sheriff come to you. We showed the sheriff our credentials. He took our names and where we were staying. We told him we were leaving in two days for Broken Arrow. We're reporting to the president of the railroad. Mr. James J. Hill was waiting in his private car on a side rail in Tulsa, which was our final destination and that we were waiting for an additional assignment, but we didn't know what it was at this point.

The sheriff said, "Bill Chestnut, seems I've read about you someplace."

I said, "I've been someplace, but I'm not wanted by the law anywhere."

He seemed satisfied with that remark. I was holding my breath to see if he had gotten any telegrams from Boston to be on the lookout for us. Evidently, he did not. We talked in small talk, and then we headed back to our hotel room; tomorrow would be busy.

Next day, the three of us split up, deciding we would see as much of the town individually as we could and put our conclusions together later. We needed to pick up some provisions for the trail. I left that job up to Will. As I had said before, he's a decent cook, if you don't care much what you say. We went into some other saloons in town, talked to the store clerks, and mainly gathered information, which might or might not be useful in the near future. You could never know too much about anything. One thing we did learn in scouting around was that the Cherokee Indian nation had a very, very large piece of land that was in high demand by all the oil companies in the vicinity. But they trusted no one. They had not signed any leases. They had heard that the tricky lawyers words put on paper would hurt them. They could not understand, and they wanted no part of dishonesty as most Indians would not tell a lie.

The next day we saddled up and headed for Tulsa. We had no idea where we were going other than the general direction, nor did we know just how far it might be. We were enjoying the countryside, and Major was ranging out ahead as he normally did; he knew his job. It was getting close to noon, and we were casually looking around for a place to put on a pot of coffee, warm up the beans, maybe soak a piece of jerky, and have some lunch.

We heard some gunshots in the distance. It seemed to me maybe a half a mile away. It was hard to tell in this flat country of Oklahoma. Of course, being nosy cowboys, we decided to check out the gunshots. We had no idea of the urgency of our quest. Major did let us know in his own way that something was happening up ahead, so we urged our horses forward a little faster. We got close to this copse of trees, close to a small stream. We could see activity happening, but we couldn't tell what was going on. As we normally did, we split up in three directions. I headed straight for the camp. Jack and Will skirted around the camp, and they were going to come in from the other sides. As I got closer to the camp, I saw two dead bodies under the trees. There were four men, and they had a girl with her top exposed and was pulling frantically at her jeans. The vision of Patricia flashed readily across my mind.

But I held my cool, slowed the horse down to a walk, raised my hands up in the air, and said, "Boys! Are we having fun yet?"

All four of the men had been so intent looking at the girl's body they hadn't heard my horse walk up, and they were startled and went for their guns—big mistake!

I whipped out the knife under the collar of my shirt and threw it as hard as I could, burying it up to the bar in the stomach of the bastard holding her shoulders. In the blink of an eye, I pulled my .45 and killed the other three. I made a point to hit all three directly in the heart so they would be no chance of survival. I guess I was thinking of Patricia. The girl was crying hysterically. Jack brought his buckskin jacket and placed it around her shoulders, hiding any exposed skin that he could. The girl was a very beautiful Cherokee Indian maiden, and we tried to reassure her as much as possible that she was safe and that we would take care of her and get her back to her people. First we must report the shooting to the sheriff, take the bodies back—the four outlaws as well as the two Indian boys that had been her companions on this trip. We moved the camp three to four hundred yards up the stream. We would take care of the trash later. Major was on guard all night to keep the predators away from the former campsite. The Indian girl had gotten her extra clothing and changed to make herself presentable. Will had tried as best he could to cook supper, and after we quieted the girl down some, she told us her story.

She said, "I am from the Blue Sky Clan of the Cherokee Indian nation. My uncle is the one and only chief of the Cherokee nation. He is my father's brother. I have gone to the university in Oklahoma City and studied Mother Earth for six years. I graduated from the University as a full-fledged geologist so I could help my tribe in its endeavor to survive. I was on my way on a scouting trip with two young men from the Blue Sky Clan, they were my companions and helpers. We had only been out two days when these four oilmen came up to our camp. They seemed to know a little about me, from the way they were speaking among themselves, and they didn't like the fact that a Native Indian could be brought into the oil business. My observation was that they were told to disrupt my trip. When they started getting rough, my two young companions protested, and they shot them both. They then seemed to catch the bloodlust in their bodies and began making advances toward me. I fought with all my strength and being, but they were too strong. Please, I must rest and try to forget this ordeal."

I picked up my bedroll and started walking down the creek to the old campsite where Major and I would spend the night protecting the bodies from predators. I built up the campfire to keep coyotes and other vermin at a distance. I rolled up inside my bedroll and tried to sleep listening to the howls and the cries of coyotes and other wild animals during the night. They made it difficult to fall asleep. I kept thinking about the atrocities of man on men and why it was so. Were horrible thoughts placed in our souls at birth? Were we, in our young years, taught these kinds of atrocities, or did we learn them all by ourselves in the dark reaches of our being? I thought about Patricia. Was I handling this properly? Another one of my mistakes. I'd have killed more men than Billy the Kid, should I ever contact her and the O'Brien family again. Did I really want to kill Tom O'Brien? So many questions and so few answers. I finally drifted off to sleep, knowing Major and his wonderful senses would awake me if trouble came in the dark of night. I wrapped myself in the dark solitude of the night and got the blessed sleep that I needed. Tomorrow would be the day of reckoning.

Next morning, I headed back up to our other camp. Will was already making breakfast of bacon and eggs that we had acquired in Broken Arrow and some potatoes. He was fixing breakfast for a queen. I guess he knew who the queen was. She was feeling much better this morning and was ready for the journey ahead. After breakfast, we two went back to the old camp, leaving the girl at the new camp there to clean up that mess and be ready to head for Broken Arrow. Our nasty, unpleasant job was to get all the bodies in the buckboard and tie to the horses and head for the sheriff's office. We arrived there a little afternoon. The deadly caravan moving slowly down the Main Street of Broken Arrow was drawing considerable attention, and hangers on followed us up the street. The sheriff had heard the noise and commotion and had come out on his porch, waiting our arrival. When he saw us, he knew something was wrong and walked out in the street.

He said, "Boys, lady, come into my office, and let's hear this out."

The sheriff sent one of his deputies down to the undertaker to come for the bodies, and we all walked in behind him to the office.

I said, "Sheriff, we found this young lady on the trail to Tulsa. She had more admirers than she could handle. I'll let her tell you the story as she told us."

"Sheriff, my name is Paula," she said, "from the Blue Sky Clan of the Cherokee nation. My uncle is the grand chief of the Cherokee nation. After six years studying at the university in Oklahoma City, I graduated with honors as an oil geologist for my people. As most people know, the Cherokee reservation has a tremendous supply of oil reserve underneath Mother Earth. I was sent to the school to learn how to manage this tremendous asset to our tribe. We had long listened to the forked tongue of the white man's lawyers, and I was doing some reconnoitering with two of my tribesmen when these oilmen invaded our camp. From overhearing their talk between themselves, I believe they were ordered to put a stop to my work and do what was necessary to discourage my mission. They started getting rough with me, and my two young companions objected, and they shot them to death. They then turned their vial treatment on me. They had me half undressed when these gentlemen heard the cries and came to my rescue. The bloodlust was up in those vile men, and they pulled their weapons on Bill Chestnut. He reacted in turn, throwing his knife into the belly of the villain that was holding me and pulled his .45 as quickly as a striking snake and killed all three in as many seconds."

The sheriff had been listening intently, and he looked over at Will and said, "Bill's a little sudden with that pistol, isn't he?"

Will looked the sheriff in the eye for seconds before he answered, and the only reply was, "Some."

I said, "Jack, take Paula to the hospital. Have them keep her overnight give her a good checkup, then come back to the sheriff's office, he will know the hotel where we are staying. Sheriff, not telling you your business, but you should notify the Cherokee Blue Sky Clan of what's happened and where their sons are. That is, Sheriff, if we're free to go. I also suggest that you go through your stack of Dodgers and see if you have any paper on any of the four. We'll talk to you later."

At the hospital where Jack took Paula, there was a reporter hanging around the emergency lobby trying to get a story; he hit the jackpot. As Paula and Jack checked in to the emergency room, he could hear some of the conversation and decided, after Paula had been taken into a private room for examination, he would speak to Jack and find out all the lurid details he could. Jack was hesitant to speak to a young reporter, but he gave a small amount of information. The next morning, out on the streets of Broken Arrow, the newspaper hawkers were yelling about the attempted attack, the killing, and some of the details. The papers were selling fast. The newspaper reporter had dug through his files and added some of our other exploits to his article, and it did make it more interesting for the readers.

We went to the hospital to check on Paula and to take her back to her people. Her injuries were minor; she had already gotten a copy of the newspaper and had read the article from top to bottom. She questioned us on why we were in Oklahoma, and we told her we were meeting James J. Hall, president of the Old Great Northern Minnesota Railroad, waiting hopefully, patiently on the side track in Tulsa in his private car.

"We had just finished an assignment in Boston and were meeting him to be reassigned. That's where we were going when we came upon your circumstances."

Paula asked about Jack Sundown.

I said, "Jack can speak very well for himself. He'll tell you his story."

Jack said, "In my very young days, I would ride with my tribe over the shining sacred mountains of North Dakota, where my ancestors lived for thousands of years. I belonged to the Lakota Sioux Knife Clan with the visionary Great War Chief Sitting Bull as our leader. I was a child playing with Sitting Bull's family, and we became friends after the battle with Custer, called the Little Bighorn, the battle of Rosebud, the battle at Greasy Grass, or whatever in legend you want to call it. We spent five or six joyous years in the sacred mountains until the great white father in Washington decided he wanted to exterminate the Sioux Indians for our yellow iron. He called on his generals to invade our lands to kill our buffalo, to starve the Indians into submission. 'The only good Indian is a dead Indian,' they said. Chief Sitting Bull, in a fighting running battle, took his tribe north to Canada, where we lived in relative peace for a few years. I was with him and grew into manhood with him, on his perilous journey. We are still great friends, as Will and Bill will attest to. I got a job after we moved to the Standing Rock Indian Reservation, on the Double O Bar Ranch in Eastern Oregon, where I met Bill and Will. We became inseparable friends. When Bill was told to leave the ranch, no fault of his, we left with him. That's my story, as it generally happened. Now we three are working as railroad detectives, going to meet Mr. Hill. By the way, my Indian name is Waaya Tonch Toiesib Kahn, believe it or not."

She laughed.

As we rode up to the sheriff's office, we could see that the townspeople had read the newspaper article also, and we were a bit of a small celebrity. The sheriff welcomed us and said he had read the newspaper and understood us more than before. He said that there was $700 reward on the outlaws that we could pick it up at the bank. I told him no; that money went to the families of the braves that were killed in the fight. We wanted no blood money on this distressing trip. We told the sheriff to get the money for Paula.

Paula's home was the old capital of the Cherokee nation. It was Tahlequah, Oklahoma. The capital was changed in 1907. We were determined to see her safely to her own clan. Jack drove Paula's buckboard, and you could see that they were getting along nicely. I was very happy for Jack and hoped that everything turned out the way we all wanted it to. We were met on the trail by some of the Blue Sky Clan, and Paula told them the complete story. They were outraged at what happened to Paula and her companions. Paula told them each of our parts and saving her and avenging the deaths of the two young braves. She gave the money pack from the bank to one of the elder braves to disperse to the boy's families. We three were hailed as heroes. Inasmuch as Paula had a large part of the clan with her now, we decided we should split trails and took the one to Tulsa to meet Mr. Hill. He had been waiting long enough. Upon arriving in Tulsa, we got a hotel room, stabled the horses, had supper, and sent a bellboy from the hotel to Mr. Hill's private car, telling him that we finally got into town and we were at his disposal. Reply was fast. He was delighted that we were here and that we should take the night off and meet him for dinner in his private car tomorrow at noon. We were thankful for the rest, which we surely needed. We went to the hotel's saloon, listened to the gossip, got our customary drinks, got Major fed, and retired to our rooms. You didn't have to rock us to sleep this night.

Next morning we went to the stables to check on our horses and to get the lay of the town. It was a long walk from the hotel to Mr. Hill's private car. So around eleven thirty, we hired a buggy to take us to his car. We had cleaned up some and didn't look like three scarecrows as we knocked on his door. The door opened, and there are the other side stood James J. Hill, not his butler. His enthusiasm and greeting us was positively sincere as he shook our hands and didn't seem to want to let go.

He showed us to the sitting room, gave us the plush chairs, pulled his chair up close to ours, and said, "I'm dying to hear your stories, what a tremendous adventure you three have performed," with which I totally agree. "I want to know it all, experience it in my own mind and heart. I have read the newspaper and know some of the last adventures. But I want to know all, every detail."

I said, "Mr. Hill the boys can speak for themselves, so I'll tell you my side of the story, and they can add in their own experiences. First of all, I owe you a thousand dollars. I cashed one of the railroad vouchers to pay for help and information in the Patricia O'Brien tragedy. I'll pay that back before I leave your car."

Mr. Hill stood up and looked me and the boys in the eye and said, "You owe me nothing, that was petty cash. When I saw that it had been cashed, I knew immediately that you needed it, and I was ready to write it off."

"Yes, sir," said Bill. "You know most of the story. I did what must be done. My side of the picture, I realize there are two sides to every story, but not to me. The authorities did not accuse me of any wrongdoing, plus all leads were circumstantial evidence. I thought I was careful not to give them solid proof, and I couldn't tell you or anyone in writing or telegram about the circumstances. I think I brought about as close to foreclosure of the incident as I possibly could. I haven't seen nor talked to anyone from the Double O Bar Ranch except my cousin, Bobby. I explained to him everything I have explained to you. I want to put in a good word for Mick Murphy, who was a great help and friend. I told the Boston-Maine railroad president that he should hire Mick and his Gandy dancer crew year round, they would be a great asset to have on our side."

Mr. Hill picked up his pen and said, "It will be done."

I continued the story until the end.

Mr. Hill said, "Bill, I am more than 100 percent on your side. I always have been. I consider what you did as an extension of my own hand that type of perversion is not to be tolerated. Oh, by the way, the newspaper just printed a small article that said Joe Edwards was found in his cell in prison, hung by his own hand."

I said, "I guess he didn't get his dignity either. We'll let Jack tell you our latest episode. It may be very interesting."

Mr. Hill said, "Jack?"

"We had finished our business in Boston and had taken the train to Tulsa. We decided that we had not worked our horses. Major was getting thicker in the middle, and we hadn't seen the country-side, that we would get off at Broken Arrow and ride the horses the rest of the way. Major was ranging ahead as he always did, and we heard shooting up ahead. I believed it was three shots. We gigged our horses a little, and they started a slow canter in that direction. As we got closer, we could make out activity up ahead but still too far away to distinguish what was happening. We then heard a woman scream-ing, and Bill suggested that we come upon the camp in three differ-ent directions. Bill went straightforward into the camp. He saw what was happening. A young Indian girl was exposed from the waist up, and two other men were trying to pull down her jeans. I don't know if you know the extent of Bill's finesse with a knife, but he pulled his knife from beneath his collar and threw it into the stomach of the one holding the girl's arms. The oilman was so intent on looking at the Indian girl they hadn't seen Bill's approach. When they did, they started pulling their guns. Bill retaliated pulled his .45 and killed all three in about three seconds. As it turns out, these oilmen had killed two of her young Indian companions who tried to protect her and were killed for their efforts. I took off my buckskin jacket, wrapped it around the Indian girl's shoulders to try and protect her as best as possible. She was hysterical, and we tried to calm her down best we could. Will, being a gourmet cook, if you don't care what you say, decided he would build a fire and cook something to eat. Maybe that would quite her down, which it did.

"She told us this story, that she is the niece of the chief of the Cherokee Blue Sky Nation. Her father is the chief's brother. That she had just spent six years in a university in Oklahoma City learning to be an oil geologist and that she passed with high scores and is now a bona fide geologist. This was her first trip at her new job, looking over the Cherokee Nation's property. We took her to the sheriff's office in Broken Arrow, turned over the bodies to the sheriff, took Paula to the hospital for a thorough overnight examination, and we stayed at a hotel until the next morning. The sheriff, the next day, said that there was a $700 bounty on these criminals that Bill had killed. Bill told the sheriff to give the money to Paula to be given to the families of the two young braves that had been killed, that he did not want blood money. Paula had not been physically harmed, and the next day we decided to take her to her family, who is of the Blue Sky Clan That's all that I can remember happening now. Maybe something will remind me later. Does that tell it all boys?" as he looked around at Will and me.

I said, "It was perfect."

Mr. Hill sat there, astounded at the story he had just been told.

He said, "I knew a long time ago that you three were the men I was searching for. Your integrity is beyond reproach. After dinner, I have something to tell you that will probably change all our lives."

His waiter came in and said, "Mr. Hill, dinner is served," and we all went out to the dining room and sat down at a round table, and it seemed as if Mr. Hill wanted to stay close to the three of us.

We had a magnificent dinner. Some of the things I ate, I didn't even know what they were, but it tasted good. One of the things that I ate was fried frog legs with some sort of yellow-looking sauce over the top; it was delicious. I had never heard of eating frog legs before in my life, but I would look forward to eating them again. Maybe it was the sauce. We had chocolate mousse for dessert. I didn't know what that was either, but it sure tasted good.

Mr. Hill said, "Men, here is what I have done, even before discussing it with you three. As you know, oil is coming of age. It's going to be the greatest boom, even larger than the gold rush. Oil will be used in not only automobiles but in factories and homes throughout the world. Whoever has control of the oil beneath the land will be an uncommonly rich person. I have had my lawyers form a company called the Great Northern oil company. This company has the power to sign oil leases to trade to do whatever is necessary in the oil business. I have listed the three of you as founding fathers of this oil company. I have issued to each of you one thousand shares of common stock and one thousand shares of preferred stock. I have funded this company with $500,000. It is in the bank here in Tulsa. As soon as you three sign your signature cards, you will be able to draw on those funds. It will take two signatures, any two of you to cash a check, most of the company will be owned by the railroad, but your shares will make each of you millionaires, many times over. It will be up to you just how big a company it will be. The more leases you sign up on good oil-bearing land, the better. This is a great trust I give you, and I know you'll honor that trust."

I said, "What a wonderful opportunity you have given us, Mr. Hill, and we certainly won't let you down, but we do have one caveat. We will not lie or speak to the Indians with a forked tongue. We will respect all people their race, origin, nationality, etc."

Mr. Hill said, "I expect nothing less from you three. You will run this business as you see fit, only to ask my advice if and when you might need it, you're on your own. You can use my carriage now to go to the bank and sign your signature cards. I'm leaving this evening for board meeting in Minnesota. Good luck."

After leaving the bank and signing the required paperwork, we went back to our hotel, went to the saloon, got a table set down, looked at each other in the eye, and said, "What a tremendous opportunity we have been given. Let's don't screw this up. This is something for us, our grandchildren, and I agree, great-grandchildren. In the many years ahead, we will come across adversaries of all types of crooks and maybe even killers. We have a responsibility to the railroad and Mr. Hill and ourselves to do the best job humanly possible, and let's reiterate among ourselves: honesty is our prime endeavor."

The next morning, eating breakfast, Jack said, "Holy smoke guys, we can't see the forest for the trees. We have just met the niece of the chief of the Cherokee nation. She is a geologist, they have vast amounts of oil-bearing land, and are looking for someone honest to develop it for them. Why can't it be us?"

Will and I looked at each other and said, "Let's get riding."

We packed our gear and was heading for Tahlequah, Oklahoma, to see Paula Blue Sky, bona fide oil geologist. It was a wonderful trip on horseback. In the last few years, we hadn't been out on the range enjoying the freedom and the beauty of the West, and of course, Major was enjoying it as well. It took us several days to reach the former capital of the Cherokee nation. We didn't try to make a lot of time; we were just enjoying the lonesomeness of the range. We knew that soon enough, civilization was going to take over and destroy what we now enjoyed. After a three-day trip, we arrived in the city of Tahlequah, Oklahoma, rested and rejuvenated. We checked in at the local hotel, took our horses to the stable, carried them down, and made them comfortable. We then went to the hotel, had our meal, and went to our rooms. As you know, on an Indian reservation, they could not sell alcoholic beverages. Of course, the bellboy could always smuggle in a quart of alcohol, if you pay him a few dollars more.

As we were having breakfast the next morning, six Indians walked up to our table. They were very polite and asked if we were the three that saved Paula Blue Sky from the ravages of the oilman.

We said, "Yes, we are."

They gave us their sincere thanks and then asked, "What are you doing on the Cherokee reservation?"

We told them that we had business to discuss with Paula Blue Sky if she would see us. They said to sit tight at the hotel, and they would get the word to Paula about us wanting to see her. I said okay. About two hours later, Paula showed up with her father, brother of the chief of the Cherokee Nation.

She greeted us warmly, especially Jack, and introduced us to her father, saying, "These are the gentlemen that got me out of that predicament."

He thanked us profusely and wanted to know what he and Paula could do for us. We told them that we had started an oil company, and we three being the founding fathers, we wanted to talk to Paula about securing her services as a geologist and get her help in guiding us to finding oil land that we could lease for production. We told them that we are three honest men who don't talk with forked tongue, who know very little about the oil business, and we need someone like Paula to help steer us in the right direction.

We told Paula and her father that we were backed by the Old Great Minnesota Railroad President, James J. Hill, and if they want verification of our rights and our bona fides, we could go to the Tulsa bank, look at the paperwork, and talk to the president of the bank—that we have full control in the amount of $500,000 capital and that we have full authority to make any lease and sign the same lease under our own conditions. This seemed to impress them both.

"We want someone who can feed us the information we need to get the oil wells in production and start paying the landowners and the oil company as fast as possible."

"Paula," said Jack, "as you know, Indians don't speak with forked tongue. If you believe me, you can believe Bill and Will, they don't speak falsely either, their word is their bond." Jack said, "I guess that's all for now, think it over and let us know."

Jack walked over to Paula's father and said, "With your and Paula's permission, I would like to call on Paula and get to know her better?"

Paula said, "I'd like that Jack," and her father only nodded his head yes.

The next morning, we were finishing our breakfast when Paula and her father came into the dining room, came up to our table, requested if they could sit, and we said, "Surely."

Paula said, "Dad and I have discussed your proposition late into the night and have come to the conclusion that, yes, I would like to work for your fledgling company. I myself am a novice in the oil business. But I have spent the last six years of my life learning the oil business out of a book. Now is the time to put what I have learned into action. I don't know how much I should be paid nor do I know what duties I will have to perform. But with the four of us, we should be able to figure this out. Father has spoken to his brother, chief of the Cherokee Nation, about you three and what you have accomplished in your young life. I believe he is open to discussion regarding signing an oil lease on the Cherokee reservation. He has been told that we believe that you are honest and will give the Cherokee a fair lease. He would like to meet with you three and myself at your earliest convenience."

"Paula," said Jack, "this is music to our ears. We too discussed your salary if you decided to work with us. We too are novices, and temporarily to start with, we thought a salary of $300 a month would be a figure to consider."

Out of the corner of my eye, I could see Paula's father do his nod yes.

She said, "All right, when do I start?" and Jack said, "You already have."

I said, "As far as meeting with your uncle, we would like to have an oil attorney meet us before the meeting so we can discuss some things and learn more about the oil business and its leases. Believe me, we want the best lease possible for your nation. Can we move the meeting with your uncle forward to about a week from now?"

Paula's father spoke up and said, "You are wise, and that will be reported to the chief."

We said, "Tomorrow, Paula, let's meet here and go find us an office location large enough that we cannot only handle the Cherokee oil lease if we're lucky enough to agree with your uncle but also other leases and other oil lands that you and we can sign up or buy."

The meeting broke up, and as Paula and her father were leaving, Jack went over and asked Paula if he could pick her up for dinner tonight.

She looked at him and said, "Jack, that would be perfect, how about eight o'clock?"

"Done," said Jack, "what's your address?"

We immediately searched out the local telegrapher. We needed to notify Mr. Hill of our progress and our need for an oil lease attorney.

We said in our telegram, "We have to be very discreet on what we say in this telegram, trust us in this endeavor, tell the attorney that we are his employers in this particular incident, that he listens to our wishes and does what we tell him to do. Great things can come out of this meeting. There are unscrupulous people with their ear to the ground, waiting to hear of any important information that they themselves can act upon much less sell the info. We need this attorney in place no later than three days from now. I know that you trust us, and we are working for the railroad and you, as well as for us. We believe we are making great strides."

The next morning, we received a telegram from Mr. Hill, saying, "Understood, done, good luck, you are writing your own ticket. As ever, Jim."

The next morning, Paula showed up just after breakfast, and we hired a cab to take us around to find our offices. We needed a very large main office for Jack, Will, and me, and then we need a medium-size office and a very large boardroom with a large desk, which should seat about ten to twelve people, and we needed a small kitchen alongside the boardroom. We might have to have that built. We found almost exactly what we were looking for in the very decent part of the business district, and we told the agent to write up a three-year lease for the space, and we would be by tomorrow or the next day to consummate the lease. In the main room was a huge stone fireplace with multicolored stones. It was very beautiful and had a stone hearth and mantel. Once furnished properly, it would make a very impressive office for our oil company. Paula approved the office layout and the location. It was close to the banks and to the courthouse for recordation of any paperwork that we needed recorded. It had been a day out for Major as well. He loved the ride in the buggy, or cab, and was looking very interestingly around. We decided that we would go by the hotel and drop me and Will off at the hotel, and Jack would take Paula on home and then return to the hotel. That was our plan. As we went back to the hotel desk to get our key, the clerk said that someone was asking about me.

"He didn't leave his name, he just requested your room number."

That seemed a little odd to Will and me, so we proceeded very cautiously toward our room. And getting closer to the room, I told Major to fetch. He immediately put his nose to the carpet and began smelling, and I knew that someone was waiting for us in our room, up to no good. We didn't know how many men were in the room, how they were armed, but it was obvious that they were there for evil purposes. I told Will that we were going to burst into the room with our guns drawn and my knife from my belt in my left hand. I was as good throwing a knife with one hand as the other. I wanted to keep one of the outlaws alive for questioning, if at all possible.

I knocked on the door of the room and said loudly, "Bellhop reporting, bellhop reporting," and a gruff voice inside the room said, "We didn't order a bellhop, leave us alone, we'll call you if needed."

We knew for certain that they were up to no good. And that he used the word *we* meant there were more than one man behind the door. It was now time to fish or cut bait. We burst through the door into the dim-lit room. It was light enough for us to see the shadows of two men in the room. Our eyes was not as accustomed to the darkness as the outlaws, so they got off the first shot. Will dropped to the floor. This was the second time he had been shot. He did manage to get off one shot, hitting one of the outlaws in the shoulder. I immediately lined the sights of my pistol on the other man's forehead and pulled the trigger. No sympathy for the man who had shot my friend, and at this point, I didn't know if he was dead or alive as he lay bleeding on the floor. The gunshots brought other people into the hallway, and a bellboy ran for the sheriff and the doctor. I bent over Will's body and checked his wounds. He had been shot high up on the right side of his chest. He was bleeding profusely, and I took my neckerchief and tried to stop the bleeding. It seemed as if they all came at once, the police from the reservation—the doctor and, of course, a reporter who smelled a story.

Will was lying on the bed. He was conscious, and he was saying quite a few colorful words. He was mad at himself because he had not done more, and I said, "Will, you did everything that you could do, and I appreciate your help."

I told the reservation police in detail what happened. Then the questions were started by the reporter; he too was asking a lot of questions. I know if I told the story about the potential lease, the word would hit Oklahoma like a huge tornado as the oil resources was a long-standing question. I did tell the reservation police that I knew Paula Blue Sky and her father, if they needed any confirmation about who we were, and that all this was confidential.

About that time, Jack came bursting into the room, saying, "My god, what's happened? I saw all the activity out front, and I couldn't wait to get here."

I told Jack what had happened in minute detail. I could hear him cursing under his breath because he wasn't here with us when we needed him.

I told Jack, "At least we know now that the telegrapher was in cahoots with whoever these bastards worked for, and with him has a witness and the one that Will winged. We should be able to get some valuable information from either of them. And I supposed the Cherokee know how to interrogate."

Jack and I followed the ambulance to the hospital, and we waited around for the surgeon to tell us his diagnosis about Will. He said the gunshot wound was not critical but very painful and would take several weeks to heal; that was very good news to Jack and me. We then got an officer from the Indian reservation, not letting any grass grow around our feet. We were going to go and pick up the telegrapher and ask him some pertinent questions, as to whom he delivered the message of our telegram. We had to do this quickly because the news was spreading fast through the city of Tahlequah, and we didn't want the telegrapher to get scared and leave town before we could pick him up. He was a vital part of our case. We picked up the telegrapher and took him to the jail. The replacement telegrapher was notified, and the office was opened. Paula, along with her father and most other residents of the city, heard the news of the gunfight and the apparent results. But most of the people of the city were surprised at the length of the article in the newspaper, depicting my and Will's and later on Jack's exploits. It was quite an article, and even Paula and her father were surprised. We were the current heroes of the reservation. The reporter used a little of the writer's prerogative in describing our talents.

He said, and I quote, "Bill Chestnut is the fastest pistolero, most accurate man west of the Mississippi, and the only way anyone could take him down would be by Bushwhack from behind."

I didn't care much for that analogy. But there it was in print, and I couldn't do anything about it. The reporter added up my kills to twenty-six. I wasn't proud of the amount; I just knew they were in self-defense for the good of the country. The Indians called me the White Warrior after that, and the name had stuck.

The lawyer arrived, and he met us at the hotel. He had gotten a copy of the newspaper and had read the entire article. He was in his late forties or early fifties and seemed to be a likable person. I believed he was a little awestruck at the three of us and what we have accomplished in our young lives. We told him we had a meeting with the chief of the Cherokee nation to discuss his tribe and our company joining in an oil lease agreement.

"The three of us want to go over the oil lease in detail, and we will have plenty of questions for you, and we want the answers to each question, even if there are two or three or four answers. We want all those also. We want to give a good, sound business lease to the Cherokee nation."

We asked Paula to come to the meetings to hear our discussions. After three days of grilling, we knew the leases well. It was time to meet the chief. We asked Paula to set up a meeting for tomorrow, if at all possible. Will was out of the hospital with his arm in a sling, but he wanted to go to the meeting; that was fine with us. I told Paula there would be five at the meeting, including her and the attorney, and if the chief wanted his counsel, please have them there also.

As we approached the chief's house, a brave met us and said, "Please follow me."

He took us around the side of the house to the backyard, and there we saw an elaborate fire pit with a medium-size fire burning, and around the fire pit we learned was the Cherokee Indian council with the chief sitting at the head. They wore their elaborate clothing and their headdresses for this occasion; it told everyone there that this was a serious council meeting. As we approached the council fire, the chief stood up. He had a peace pipe across his arm, and his head-dress flowed to the ground with multicolored feathers from birds I didn't even know existed, and maybe they didn't now. Each council person had on his best. He put his hand up in the sign of peace, and I did the same.

He said, "Do I speak to the White Warrior?"

I said, "I have been honorably given that name, but my real name is Bill Chestnut."

He bowed and motioned for all of us to sit around the fire.

He said, "This is a serious thing we do, and it must be done to the satisfaction of the Great Spirit. We have heard many good things about you three men. You have saved my niece from the cruel oilmen, you have seen to her health, you have given her a job when she is freshly out of college, you have put your lives in danger by just talking to me and my counsel.

"There have been many forked tongues by the white man wanting to lease our land for oil, but we have resisted them. We were waiting to find honest oil agents, and it remains to be seen if we have found one now. If we don't come to an agreement, we still hold you in high honor for what you have done so far. We know most of your earlier exploits, it is a warrior's legacy."

He took his pipe and loaded it with tobacco, took a fire stick out of the council fire, and lit the pipe. He raised the pipe to the four directions of the wind and passed it to the left to the next counsel man, and so it went, and he took a small puff and blew the smoke to the four winds and passed the peace pipe to the left, to the next counsel person. That was done to each person that was sitting around the council fire. He then handed the pipe to a woman who came out of his house and said, "Let the discussions began."

The attorney who represented the Cherokee tribe came out of the house and joined our counsel.

I said, "Great Chief, we are here to explain oil leases as best we can. Your niece Paula is in attendance as well, as is your attorney. We want to begin this discussion, saying we only want a true and fair lease for the Cherokee Nation and our oil company. Everyone here understands to make a satisfactory deal, all must make a profit, we all understand that. For the last three days, my friends and I, along with Paula, have sequestered ourselves in our hotel room with this attorney and have gone over the leases with a fine as a fine toothed comb. We have asked him many, many questions, and he will answer your questions as the evening goes by. He will answer them truthfully, as he has been instructed. As I am new to this negotiation business, I will give you the best offer that I can give you first. I don't like haggling with friends. My offer is this, with the signing of a satisfactory oil lease with the Cherokee Nation, I will render a certified check to the nation in the amount of $250,000, which will be deducted from your royalties over ten years. This money is yours to do with as you please. We will agree to start production as soon as possible, no later than one and a half years from now. This lease will cover all of the Cherokee Nation's reservation. We realize that you have buildings and will work to the best of our ability to secure the oil from beneath the buildings without their destruction, if at all possible. We know how the Indian cherishes Mother Earth, and we will do our best to leave the land undisturbed and repaired. We will guarantee the Cherokee Nation 21 percent of the profits from the oil wells. If we believe there is oil deeper into the soil, it will cost more money to secure the oil, so the Cherokee percentage will drop to 18 percent we are sharing the cost. If we believe there is deeper oil, and we must drill deeper to secure the oil, the Cherokee percentage will again drop to 15 percent. I will leave it up to the attorney and your council to fill in the details of the lease. The monetary value is the important parts of the lease. Do you have any questions for me or for the attorney?"

The Indian chief stood up and looked at each of his counsel at a steady gaze, waiting a minute for each to speak if necessary. I watched as he turned to each member, and each nodded his head yes. I didn't know what the nod really meant, but I had an idea; and after the last counsel person was called upon, the chief turned his head toward me and said, "Bill Chestnut, you do not lie. I have polled the council, and they have agreed to sign your lease. There is one stipulation that you sign the lease, Bill Chestnut, also known as the White Warrior."

I said, "It's done."

I turned to my attorney and said, "Get with the tribe's attorney, and work out the details, and bring the lease no later than day after tomorrow. I want to read it so we can wrap up signatures and get the notaries, everyone necessary to consummate this lease."

"Yes, sir," he said.

Everything went smoothly, and the lease was signed by all concerned and recorded at the courthouse, so everything was public. You would think that a bomb or dynamite had exploded when the word got out the Cherokee had signed an oil production lease and had given it to the great Minnesota Railroad Company.

A telegram was sent to President James J. Hill by the company attorney, saying, "Everything is accomplished here. This lease could not have been signed but for Bill Chestnut (White Warrior). The Indians hold him in the highest esteem."

Telegram came back from Mr. Hill, saying, "I knew he could do it. It is a feather in his hat and a great honor for our railroad, give him my highest praise."

I told Will and Jack, as soon as the oil wells went into production on the Cherokee reservation, our stock in the company would be worth millions of dollars for each of us. We started getting inquiries immediately, sent from other landowners in the Oklahoma territory. If the Cherokee Indians could trust us, then they wanted to discuss oil leases with us also. Within six weeks, we were able to sign up five more leases—all with Bill Chestnut, also known as White Warrior, signature. More money was wired into our bank in Tulsa for earnest money.

As the news of our extremely good fortune got to Mr. Hill, he decided he wanted the three of us, including Paula and her father and the Cherokee chief, to come to the headquarters of the Old Great Minnesota Railroad and receive a bonus for our extraordinarily good work and luck.

I wired Mr. Hill that maybe when we get there, we could have a wedding. "I believe Jack and Paula are ready to tie the knot. It could be a wonderful occasion."

I decided to write Bobby a letter and fill him in on all the circumstances.

Dear Bobby, a few words to say, about Will, Jack, and me. On our way to Tulsa, we stopped some oil men from raping a young Indian maiden. She is the niece of the chief of the Cherokee nation. I had to kill a couple of oilman out of self-defense. The oilmen had killed two braves already. The Indians then held us in very high esteem they have named me White Warrior.

Will, Jack, and I formed an oil company and worked out an oil lease for the Cherokee strip. Jack, Will, and I would like to pick you up in Arlington in our railroad car and take you with us for the festivities. If you can get away from the ranch, I can fill you in at that time about the further escapades that we have had and are continuing to have. We have missed you a lot. I realize that things can't stay the same forever and that each of us must walk down our own paths to our own destiny. Please let me know by telegram at this return address if you can make the connection.

Two days later, a telegram came from Bobby, saying, "I'll be there, wire date and time. I may bring a friend. But that's an entirely different story. Your cousin, Bobby."

About the Author

Jack was raised on a thirty-acre farm in Central Kentucky. At age seventeen, he hoboed to Fossil, Oregon, where he worked in the lumber business as a pond monkey. He quit the lumber business to work at the Muddy Company ranch in Eastern Oregon, which is 250,000 acres. His next journey was in Ohio, where he was a baker. He moved back to Kentucky and married his high school sweetheart at age nineteen. He served in the US Army as a master sergeant during the Korean War. He turned down a battlefield commission as a first lieutenant. He spent four years and nine months in the service of his country. Jack has two children, a boy named Bartley and a girl named Tina. He is in the real estate business in Phoenix, Arizona, and he now lives on a small horse ranch in North Phoenix.

CPSIA information can be obtained
at www.ICGtesting.com
Printed in the USA
FFHW022349210619
53140877-58817FF